Praise for THE SUMMER I BECAME A NERD

"Between the laugh out loud dialogue and Maddie and Logan's

who wants to let her nerd flag fly. I highly recommend it."
- Just a Couple More Pages

the summer
i became a
neRd

the summer i became a

neRd

leah rae miller

Entangled Publishing, LLC
2614 South Timberline Road
Suite 109
Fort Collins, CO 80525

Visit our website at www.entangledpublishing.com.

Edited by Heather Howland and Sue Winegardner
Cover design by Heather Howland

Ebook ISBN   978-1-62061-239-2
Print ISBN   978-1-62061-238-5

Manufactured in the United States of America

First Edition May 2013

For my parents, Clyde and Nancy.

prologue

When I was in junior high, the school I went to held a Halloween festival every year in the gym. There were all these little booths where we could bob for apples or throw darts at balloons for crappy little prizes like plastic spider rings and whistles that didn't work. There was a "jailhouse" that was really just a big cardboard box with a door and a window with black spray-painted PVC pipes as the bars. We could pay a dollar to send someone to "jail" for one minute. For some reason this turned into a declaration of love if a boy sent a girl to jail.

The biggest part of this festival was always the costume contest, probably because the winner actually won cash. In sixth grade, I was determined to win this contest. I spent weeks before the festival making my costume. I figured if I went as something the judges—who were just the softball coach, the head of the cafeteria, and the principal—had never seen before, I was sure to win.

At the time, I was really into this comic book series called The Pigments. My favorite character was Spectrum Girl. She had a pink afro and this awesome cape. The cape was what I spent most of my time on. I got these long, wide strips of fabric in every shade of the rainbow, then lined the edges of each strip with bendable wire so the strips would stick out behind me and be all wavy so it would look like I was flying.

On the night of the festival I was so pumped I almost threw up as I waited in the wings of the stage. The other competitors had all chosen the same old costumes: witch, robot, the main character of whatever the most recent animated movie was. I could feel it in my very core that I had this thing wrapped up.

Then, Mrs. Birdhill announced me.

"Our next trick-or-treater is Maddie Jean Summers. She's dressed as" — and here's where I started to doubt myself because when she said this last part, it sounded like she was reading words she had never heard before — "the leader of the superhero team The Pigments, Spectrum Girl?"

Yep, she ended it like she was asking a question.

I stepped onto the stage, expecting a wave of *ooh*s and *ahh*s, but what I got was complete silence. I swear I heard a cricket chirp somewhere in the back of the room when I stepped up to the microphone.

"Hi. I spent two weeks working on my costume. I chose Spectrum Girl because she's the strongest of all the Pigments, and I think she sets a great example for young women today," I said and took a few giant steps back so I could make a slow turn.

When I made the complete 360, I stopped and looked out at

the audience. It was a sea of my peers, everyone I went to school with, everyone I wanted desperately to impress. In the front row was my best friend, who shall remain nameless. She would always rag on me when I mentioned anything comic related, so I had learned not to talk about it.

I remember looking down at her in her cheerleader costume. I'm sure my eyes were pleading with her to break the silence, to help me—even if she didn't like comics, we were best friends. Surely she'd support me.

Instead, she leaned over to the girl next to her and whispered something in her ear. They both giggled before she-who-shall-not-be-named yelled, "Where did you get your costume idea?"

I stepped up to the microphone, thinking my answer would help. Everyone loves Superman and Batman, how could they not like a costume based on a comic character?

"The Pigments is a comic book I like a lot," I said.

"A comic book? What a dork!"

I don't know if everyone agreed with her, but they all laughed with her. Laughed me right off the stage. Thank goodness no one was hanging out by the back exit because it would have been even more embarrassing if someone had caught me bawling my eyes out in a dark corner.

Later, as I tore my excellently crafted cape to shreds and stuffed it into a garbage bag, I vowed no one would ever get the chance to hurt me like that again.

And that's when my double life began.

#1

Louisiana summers are unforgiving. Or maybe I'm too freaking impatient to tolerate the usual ninety-six-degrees-in-the-shade heat. The final book in The Super Ones comic book series, which I've been obsessing over for years, comes out today, and I'm waiting for Randy Henderson from down the street to finish mowing our lawn so I can check the mailbox. Normally, I download my comics and read them on the computer so there's no physical proof of my secret life, but the author of this particular series has insisted the final book only be available in print.

Hurry up, Randy. Except, I think my impatience has made things worse. I'm pretty sure he thinks I'm checking him out. Every few minutes, he sends me a sideways glance from where he sits atop his riding mower and tries his best to do a crooked grin like he's Robert Pattinson or something. I bet he's practiced it in the mirror. I hope he doesn't hit on me tomorrow at school. Eric, my boyfriend, has never actually hurt someone for checking me out. He's usually too busy being a "dude-bro." It's all about football and chicks and "dude-bro, we should totally go mud riding this weekend." But catching Randy checking me out would be a chance to cause physical harm which, let's face it, is what football is mostly about. And Eric is good at football.

Finally, Randy rounds the large pecan tree in our front yard, cutting the final patch of grass, and heads down our driveway. As he turns right onto the street to go home, he waves back at me, revealing a thick mass of dark, curly underarm hair. Did you know smiling suppresses the gag reflex? I do, so I smile and wave back.

Once the sound of the lawn mower is barely audible, I jump up and run off the porch. Maybe it's more of a sprint. A dash? Either way, I manage to get to the mailbox and pull out the contents with near-inhuman speed. As soon as I spot the manila envelope, I swear angels sing. I super-run back to the house and dump all the mail on the kitchen counter, except for the manila envelope. I take the stairs to the second floor in leaps and bounds. Grabbing the frame of my door before I fly past it, I use my momentum to swing into my room. The door slams closed behind me.

I throw the envelope onto the bed, not wanting to look at it until I'm ready. This is too important to simply breeze through the moment. I dig out my comic journal from its hiding place in the closet—on the top shelf, stuck inside a stack of sweaters that won't be brought out until early December—and throw it on the bed, as well. It's just a notebook where I keep all my thoughts about the books I read, but to me it's a treasure trove of secret identities, quotes, and life lessons only superhumans can teach.

I kick off my flip-flops a little too hard and they hurtle through the room, almost knocking over my bedside lamp. Whoops. I twist my blond hair into a messy bun on the top of my head. Can't have any tendrils escaping while I'm reading and blocking my view.

This is it. Is Marcus, The Sonic One, strong enough to defeat Baron Gravity? Or will he be sucked into oblivion by one of Baron Gravity's randomly created black holes? Will Wendy realize she loves Marcus and fly to his rescue? Does Grayson, the lovable but oblivious sidekick also known as The Young One, die, thereby making me cry because he never found out the true identity of his parents?

I sink into my plush comforter and cross my legs under me. I pull off the purple pen that's been hanging onto the spiral wire binding of my comic journal, turn to a blank page, and write: *The Super Ones* #400.

I am ready.

Eyes closed, I pick up the envelope. I blindly feel for the flap, open it, and pull out the comic. It's thin, but oh-so-crisp. There's nothing better than the smell of fresh ink, so I take a deep breath to lock away the memory of this moment. After making sure I have it facing the correct way by fingering the pages with my right thumb and sliding the tip of my left index finger over the staples binding it, I take another deep breath, then open my eyes.

YOUR ORGANIC GARDEN AND YOU

Huh?

I throw my comic journal off my lap and lean over the side

of the bed to grab the discarded envelope. Nothing else in there. There are only regular envelopes on the kitchen counter. I couldn't have missed it.

I scramble to my desk and turn on my laptop, barely resisting the urge to call it a slow piece of junk and cursing myself further. I pull up my e-mail, which I haven't checked since I got home from school, because I had been too busy watching Randy do his Robert Pattinson impression. Sure enough, there's an e-mail.

Dear Madelyne Jean Summers,

Due to unprecedented demand, *The Super Ones* #400 is currently out of stock. Your copy will be shipped in 5-7 weeks. We apologize for the inconvenience.

They apologize? Are they kidding?! I can't wait five to seven weeks. I must know now! Can Wendy, a.k.a. The Bright Frenzy, man-up and tell her father to get a life so she can fly off to the war-ravaged planet of Zocore in order to sacrifice herself in the ensuing battle? Will Marcus make a dying attempt to block a severe radiation blast heading straight for Young One's face?

It's too much to deal with. I must get my hands on issue #400.

There's only one place in town that would have a copy. Is the risk of being seen and losing my place atop Natchitoches Central's elite worth it? No. Absolutely not. It's been a long, hard climb to the top of the popularity ladder. It took a lot of deceit and subterfuge to get people to forget The Costume Incident. And once something like that is started, there's no going back. I've been at it for five years now. Not having anyone to geek out with over the latest superhero movie (other than my brother, but he doesn't count), having to hold my tongue about all my fandoms, making a mad dash to hide all nerdy evidence every time a friend shows up at my house unannounced... I'm in a constant state of "no one can know," and it sucks.

But...can I go two months without knowing? Can I last two months without going on the comic book forums, Twitter, or Facebook for fear of spoilers?

Of course I can't.

Damn your awesomeness, Super Ones.

I grab a hoodie, my dad's green Boston Celtics cap, and I make double sure my shades are in my purse.

Drastic times call for drastic measures.

#2

There it is. The Phoenix.

You know how some people say Paris is one of their favorite places even though they've never been there? The Phoenix is like that for me.

An image of a yellow and orange flaming bird hangs above the door, and through the windows I can see row upon row of comics in all their Mylar-encased glory. I don't know how many times I've driven by here and almost rear-ended someone because I was trying to ogle the newest life-size cardboard cutout of Wolverine or Captain America or whoever.

And now I'm here. Of course, I'm not actually parked in their parking lot. I'm technically in the Mes Amis lot next door. My friends and I love this restaurant but for different reasons. My best friend, Terra, loves the low-fat cheesecake. Eric loves the double bacon cheeseburger. I love the fact that I can see the display windows of The Phoenix from our usual booth.

I turn my car off since I don't have an air conditioner. It's just blowing hot air in my face, making me sweat like I'm about to do a toe-touch off the top of the pyramid at halftime. I put on my dad's cap, my big, retro sunglasses, and my sunshine-yellow hoodie. Satisfied with my incognito ensemble, I jump out of the car and duck between the other vehicles to sneak my way to the small, shaded alley separating Mes Amis and The Phoenix.

I set up camp and wait. If I peek around the edge of the building, I can see The Phoenix's front door, but no one is coming in or out. I wait some more, passing the time by doing a little positive visualization: me, sitting in my air-conditioned room with *The Super Ones* #400 in my hands.

Just then, I hear someone pull up.

Out of the small Toyota Corolla steps a guy, probably in his thirties. He's balding and has a stain on his red T-shirt. Before he can make it to the door, I let out a loud, "Psst!"

He stops and looks around, then notices me. I wave him over and duck back down the alley. After a second, his head appears around the corner, one eyebrow raised. "Yes?"

"Want to earn five bucks for two minutes of work?" I try to sound as unconcerned as possible.

"What do you want?"

"I give you money, you go in there"—I shove a thumb at the wall behind me—"and buy me a copy of *The Super Ones* #400. You get the change and five extra bucks. Deal?" I stare at him over the tops of my sunglasses.

"Why don't you buy it yourself?"

"I just can't, okay? So, do we have a deal?"

"Make it ten dollars, plus the change." He crosses his arms like he's haggling at a swap meet.

My mouth drops open. "But I don't have any more cash. Just ten dollars, three dollars for the book, leaving seven dollars for you. Come on!"

"Nothin' doin'." He shakes his head and walks away.

The bell rings as he goes inside, and I flop against the brick wall of the store. What a jerk!

"It's okay," I say out loud. "Someone else will be by any second."

After a few minutes, the bell rings again, and I hear, "Psst."

The guy is standing there with a thin paper bag. The Phoenix's emblem blazes across it. He slowly pulls out a comic, lifts the plastic flap, and presses his nose to the opening. He takes a deep whiff.

"Ahhhh," he says as he releases the breath. "Pictures and words. All that brand new ink. It's intoxicating."

"What is that?" I blurt out and take a deep breath, too, hoping somehow that beautiful smell will reach me.

"*The Super Ones* #400." He smiles and puts it back in the paper bag.

"Just show me the cover, please," I say as he unlocks his car door.

"Sorry. No time. I have reading to do." Before he leaves, though, he rolls down his window and yells, "You might want to man up and go in there. There's only one copy left."

My heartbeat speeds up, and my palms start to sweat even more. *Is it worth the risk?* I ask myself as I begin to pace.

It's not like any of my friends are going to come in, and I'm thoroughly disguised even if someone I knew did happen to be in there.

Only one copy left.

I have to take the chance.

I take a fortifying breath and square my shoulders before I stroll up to the glass door of The Phoenix.

I can't believe it. The Phoenix. I'm about to go into The Phoenix!

I pull the door open, and the twinkly bell I heard from the alley sounds above me. The store is set up like a book itself. I'm standing at the end of a long empty walkway. On both sides of me, metal, A-frame racks are lined up like pages waiting to reveal their awesomeness. Spinning racks are scattered throughout the store. Collectable action figures mint-in-the-box and key chains featuring superhero logos dangle from the racks' hooks. One spinning rack is covered top to bottom with slim foil packages containing *Magic: The Gathering* playing cards. If I wasn't trying to be sneaky about this whole thing, I'd give that rack of commons, uncommons, and rares a big ole whirl just to see the shimmery packets reflect the summer sunlight filtering through the windows.

"Welcome to The Phoenix, can I help you find anything?" a guy's voice asks from the end of the walkway.

Keeping my head down, I dart down one of the aisles on my left. "Just looking," I say and then snort at my own silly attempt to sound like a man.

"Let me know if you need any help."

There's a hint of suspicion is in his voice, but I stay hidden. Superspeed would be handy right now. I could find my book and leave the money on the counter without being seen. "Okay."

Then, I get lost. Lost in the bright colors of the covers, lost in the stacks and stacks of lovely, numerically organized issues. The comics are grouped by publisher and alphabetically by series. There's Marvel's Ant-Man next to The Avengers. Booster Gold and Blue Beetle from DC. By the time I come across Fables, my number three favorite Vertigo title, I've run out of shelves on this side. I zip across the empty aisle and try to focus on the task at hand. The Super Ones must be somewhere in the middle of these shelves. There's Sandman, Superman, ah ha, The Super Ones.

I slide out the last comic in the stack.

#399?

I search the surrounding stacks, thinking maybe that money-exploiting jerk hid it from me, but I can't find it.

Here's the part where any normal person trying not to be recognized would give up and leave. Actually, a normal person wouldn't have disguised themselves in the first place, but that's a whole other matter. I, being a very nonnormal person, am going to have to ask the cashier and hope he's some college kid that won't give me a second look.

I take another fortifying breath and walk up to the counter. The guy is bent so far over a comic I can only see the top of his head, which is covered with brown, messy hair. I make an "ahem" noise to get his attention, but he doesn't look up. I raise my sunglasses up a little to glance at the book he's reading. I see a full splash page of Marcus. His whole body is contorted in agony as he screams—and I know he's screaming because the speech bubble next to his head is all pointy—"NOOOOOO!!!!" I squeeze my eyes shut, not wanting the book to be spoiled for me, but the damage is already done. I'm at the end of my rope.

"Do you have a copy of *The Super Ones* #400?" I say, abandoning my faux-guy voice.

He finally looks up, and I recognize him. Not only do I recognize him, I *know* him. I could probably tell you what shoes he's wearing (black and white chucks with frayed laces) even though his lower half is hidden behind the counter. I know this because he's kind of been my geek idol for a while now and I've…paid attention.

Last year, he got in trouble at school because he was wearing pornography. At least, that's what the students were told, when in reality, he was just wearing a T-shirt sporting an Adam Hughes drawing of Power Girl. Ridiculous, I know. I mean, Adam Hughes is one of the best purveyors of the female form in comics today, even if he has a tendency to overexaggerate certain body parts.

Ever since then, I've had a thing for Logan Scott. Not an actual *thing* since I have a boyfriend and that would be bad, but he's got these cute freckles on his nose and cheeks, probably from playing soccer—he's the Natchitoches Central High School's goalie—and he's always reading, comics mostly, but every once in a while, I'll catch him with a high fantasy book with dragons or elves on the cover. Not that I'm stalking him or anything.

He has really nice eyes, though.

His brow furrows when he looks at me. "Sorry, we're all out."

"Really? What's that?" I point at the book he's currently stuffing under the counter.

"It's…" He trails off as he takes in the way I'm dressed. He tilts his head to the side like he's trying to see behind me. I whip around, thinking someone else is there, but the store is still empty. When I turn back, a knowing smile plays at the edges of his mouth. Sighing right now would be bad, but he has perfect boy-lips—not too full, not too thin.

He props his chin on his fist. "Do I know you?"

"Uh, no, I mean, I don't think so. I'm just passing through town. I mean, I don't live here or anything so how could you know me?" I say in a rush.

"Okay." He squints like he can pull a confession out of me with his eyes alone. "That's too bad, because this is the last copy."

He pulls #400 out and waves it around, which sends electricity shooting through me because: (1) it's right in front of my face, and I can see the amazing cover, and (2) the way he's flopping it around is breaking the spine, which breaks my heart. You'd think a guy who works at a comic shop would be a little more careful.

Instinct kicks in, and I throw out my hands like he has a gun pointed at a puppy. He stops and lays the book on the counter between us.

"Why is it too bad?" I ask. "I'm a paying customer. I give you money, you give me #400. That's how these things work." I tentatively reach for #400, but he slaps his hand down flat on top of it.

"It's too bad you're just passing through, don't live here, and don't know me, because this is my copy, and if you *weren't* just passing through, lived here, and knew me, I might let you borrow it."

He smiles that knowing smile, and more of that electricity shoots through my body, but for completely different reasons: (1) that smile is the irresistible kind I can't help but return, and (2) his voice has a soft, smooth quality that makes my brain turn to jelly.

I shake these thoughts from my mind when a voice in the back of my head shouts, "Quarterback boyfriend!"

"Well, by passing through, I meant visiting. I'll probably be around for the next couple of days so I could have it back to you pretty quick."

He scratches the back of his neck. "Hmm."

"I promise," I blurt out, my hands clasped together. I can't believe I've been reduced to begging. "I'll have it back to you in a couple of hours even."

There's that smile again. He might be adorkable, but he's not being very nice, teasing me like this.

"We'll be closed in a couple of hours, so I'll give you my number, and you can call me when you're done."

"Perfect. No problem at all." I nod again and again until I think I've given myself whiplash.

He presses a button on the cash register, and blank receipt paper rolls out of the slot on the top. He hands me #400. I devour the cover with my eyes as he rips the receipt paper off and jots down his number. When he reaches for the book again, I jerk it away, thinking *Mine!*

"I just want to put this in there so you don't lose it," he says slowly, like he's trying to calm a hostile beast.

"Oh." I hand him the book. He slides the piece of paper behind the last page. "Can I get a bag? I don't want it to get any sun damage."

The bag might be another piece of evidence I'll have to find a hiding place for, but I might never have the guts to come back to The Phoenix. I want a memento, darn it.

#3

That was incredible! No, it was amazing! Incredizing? Amazible? Whatever. It was awesome, the perfect ending to a spectacular series. Of course, the story was left a little open at the end to allow for future spin-offs and things, but that's to be expected.

I turn the final page of #400 to read the "Letter from the Author" and the receipt paper with Logan's number on it slides into my lap. I don't look at it until I'm completely done reading every last word of the author's "this couldn't have happened without the fans" thing.

I write down my final thoughts in my comic journal, ending with a quote from the book: *Be true to yourself and others will be true to you, too.* It's a nice thought, but so not realistic.

Now that I'm done, I can return the book and forget I almost exposed my dark side to another living person. I'm about to dial the number on the slip of paper when I read what else he wrote:

I know your secret identity.

"He *what?*" I jump off my bed, still staring at the note.

How could he know who I am? I was adequately disguised. I told him I didn't live in this town.

This is a disaster.

What do I do? Call him up and pretend like I have no idea what he's talking about? Try to bribe him to keep his mouth shut? I find myself glaring at #400 like this is all its fault but quickly look away, mentally apologizing to the book.

He's expecting me to call him tonight. He's probably sitting by his phone with that knowing smile spread across his perfect boy-lips.

My phone rings, and I jump about four feet in the air. He couldn't wait for me to call? He just had to rub it my face as soon as possible that I'm just like him and don't have the guts to admit it? Of course, this is true, but it's not polite to rub anything in anyone's face unless it's… Well, now that I think about it, it's never polite.

I lean over, eye the screen on my phone, then relax. It's just Terra. I should have known. We have a standing appointment of a thirty minute phone call every night.

I lucked out when it comes to Terra. She's awesome, plus she moved here after The Costume Incident. We've been best friends since ninth grade, cheer-sisters since tenth grade, and soul-sisters since we were born. Or, at least, that's what we've decided. We are proof positive that opposites attract. Where I'm stand-offish and shy, she's charismatic and balls-to-the-wall outgoing. I mean, seriously, who has inside jokes with their English teacher? The girl could make friends with an armadillo. And I'm so thankful she's as awesome she is. Without her, I wouldn't be where I am today.

"Hey, Terra."

"Oh my God, Maddie, did you hear?" she asks, and my breath hitches.

Someone knows. Someone saw me leaving with that bag or talking to Mr. More Money.

"Hear what?" I ask in a weak voice.

"Allison Blair is doing a concert in Shreveport next month!" she screams, and I let out a sigh of relief.

"Cool, very cool," I lie. Like most people around this area, I like country music, and Allison Blair is the biggest thing to hit the country music scene in years. But I just don't get it. Her songs are too sappy with no meat to them, and they're so overplayed. All of my friends love her to bits. Little, tiny, microscopic bits. Which is why I have both of her CDs strategically placed on the backseat so everyone thinks I'm a fan when they pass my car.

The things I do to fit in.

"So?" Terra prods.

"So?"

"So, are we going? I have to go, I mean, when will we ever get this chance again?"

Actually, we'll probably get this same exact chance next year or the year after that or, hell, maybe in a few months, considering how often these tours happen, but I don't tell her that.

"I don't know. I'll have to ask my parents." I look at Logan's note again. How can I think of an adequate excuse to not go to this concert when I hold my potential downfall in my hand? It's just a simple one sentence note, you might say, but I see it for what it really is.

A threat.

"Well, ask them. Tickets go on sale in two weeks, and people are going to snatch them up. If I find some good ones, I'll grab you one, okay?"

"Yeah, sounds great." I'll figure out some way to get out of this later. At the moment, I have bigger fish to fry. When Terra hangs up, I drop my phone on my bed and crush Logan's note in my hand.

• • •

I pull into a parking space and glance in the rearview mirror at Natchitoches Central High School. It's the last day of school. Today, I officially become a senior. I should be strutting through the halls like a peacock, eying soon-to-be juniors and bestowing my newly gained seniorly wisdom upon them, but instead, I'm sitting here in my hand-me-down Lumina wondering if Logan really knows who I am.

This could be a disaster of epic proportions. What if he says something to someone? What if the girls on the squad realize I swoon over Peter Parker or that I secretly wish our uniforms included a cape? It would be The Costume Incident all over again. Good-bye awesome plans for this summer. Good-bye stress-free senior year.

If he puts the word in the right person's ear, the double life I've been leading for five years will crumble like a fortune cookie beneath the Hulk's big, green toe.

It's not that all my friends have an unnatural hatred of comic books. It's just one of those things popular people like me aren't supposed to be into. We're not like the group of poor RPG-obsessed guys that meet every morning in the band room to get in some imaginary life-living before class. They, at least, aren't too embarrassed to admit who they are and what they love.

I envy them.

When I walk into first period, Logan is sitting behind my normal desk even though his regular seat is in the back row, third from the window. He doesn't say a word, but I can feel him staring at me. The back of my neck stays warm through the whole class like he has heat vision. Which puts me even more on edge. It's like he's toying with me. Or maybe he really doesn't know. Please, please, please let him not know.

My second class period goes by without a hitch. During lunch, though, things get stressful.

"Dude, did you read #400 yet?" a boy's squeaky voice says behind me in the lunch line. It's hard not to know the owner of that voice: Dan Garrett.

"Unfortunately, no," Logan says, his voice a complete contrast to Dan's, all velvety and shiver inducing. He raises his voice a little. "I lent my copy to somebody before I finished."

Dan gasps. "Are you bat-shit crazy? It was fan-freaking-tastic."

"She seemed pretty desperate. Who am I to deny a damsel in distress?"

"She? *She*? A girl wanted to borrow your #400? Where in hellfire-damnation do you find these chicks?"

Well, at least he's creative with his expletives. Wait, did he just say "chicks" as in plural? Maybe he didn't mean another chick, specifically…

"Or was she, ya know, not hot? I mean, the old ball and chain was damn fine, and it would be cosmically unfair if you were struck with the hot-nerd-girl-lightning twice."

My ears perk up at this. He *did* mean another specific chick, but the more important matter is: does Logan Scott think I'm hot?

It gets really quiet behind me until I hear a pained grunt from Dan just as I'm paying for my food. I turn to leave and see Dan clutching his shoulder. His dirty blond hair brushes the tops of his glasses, and his mouth looks like he could be saying, "Ow, ow, ow," but the only sounds coming out are high-pitched squeaks. I glance at Logan. He's looking at the ceiling, hands clasped behind his back, whistling.

Whistling.

If there was even a little doubt in my head about whether or not Logan really knew it was me at The Phoenix, it's vanished now. My heart speeds up when he has the nerve to look me in the eyes and say, "The Celtics have a good chance at the championship this year, don't you think, Maddie?"

This is it. My tumble down the popularity ladder has begun. What if he follows me to my table? What if he asks in front of everyone if I'm done with #400 yet?

What if he never says my name in that sexy voice of his again?

Bolting for the exit doors is really tempting. I could have just realized I left my headlights on this morning. Maybe I've just come down with an incredibly rare and contagious disease.

But that would just bring more attention to the whole situation, wouldn't it?

Crap.

Logan leans forward, one eyebrow raised mischievously, waiting for my response. Instead of deigning to answer him, I edge around him and go to my regular table, head down and shoulders scrunched up. Like somehow that might keep me from being seen. Eric has saved a seat for me, but before I sit, I look out over the sea of jabbering students for Logan. Just as I find him walking to his own usual table on the other side of the cafeteria, he looks directly at me. He raises that eyebrow again and puts on that knowing smile. I avert my gaze and sit down as fast as I can.

Unfortunately, I sit on something that's moving. I squeal and jump back up, jarring the table, which knocks over Terra's bottle of water. When I look at my seat, Eric's hand wiggles its fingers at me, and he starts to laugh with great big, honkin' snorts that echo above the other commotion.

Another quick glance at Logan and he's shaking his head. I slap Eric's muscled upper arm and say, "You're such a jerk," in my most I'm-a-giggly-cheerleader voice, but what I really want to do is dump my fifty-cent banana pudding on his tall, dark, and handsome head.

"Seriously, Eric, grow up," Terra says as she mops up her water with some napkins.

"Whatever, that was classic!" He fist-bumps Peter.

"You going to the party tonight, Maddie?" Terra asks.

"Sure, I guess." I look over at Eric. "Are we going?"

"Hell, yes," he says through a mouth full of spaghetti, and I can't stop my nose from scrunching up at the sloppy sound of the food vibrating in his mouth. Gross.

And that was the most important part of the conversation because the rest of lunch was spent listening to Eric and Peter discuss their upcoming summer vacation to Destin, Florida. If you could call it a vacation. It sounded more like Jocks Gone Wild with all the "getting wasted" with Peter's brother and the "hot babes" that are sure to be on the beach. This last part was supposed to be whispered, but Eric is kind of like a four-year-old in a seventeen-year-old's body. He doesn't quite understand the concept of voice volume control.

There was no "I'll miss you so much, Maddie-babe," or "I'll call you every night," like a normal boyfriend would have said. Not that I expected that from him, or even wanted it.

I know I'm just an accessory to him, but what he doesn't realize is he's just a handbag to me, too. He's not a bad guy. Despite his immaturity, he does most of the required boyfriend things. He puts his arm around my shoulders when we walk down the hall, he points to me when he makes a touchdown-scoring pass—after he points to the stands, of course—and he never chats up other girls in my presence. There's just something missing. I don't get *that* feeling. You know, the swoony one a girl is supposed to get when she sees her guy waiting for her by her locker in the morning. But what can I do? Landing Eric as a boyfriend was the coup de grace of completing my nonnerdy persona. The quarterback dates the cheerleader. This is the way things are supposed to be.

#4

The last day of school finishes up with the customary trashing of the halls with all the papers previously buried in people's lockers, which I don't do because the school janitor is a nice guy.

I take a detour on my way home past The Phoenix, and my thoughts quickly stray to Logan. I wonder if he'll be at the end-of-school party tonight, then quickly scold myself for thinking about another guy, even though the first guy is just a handbag.

I pull into my driveway right after my dad. Before I even turn off my car, he's at the window, a grin as big as Texas spread across his face.

"So? How does it feel?" he asks as he opens my door.

"How does what feel?"

"To be a senior? Big man on campus now." He squeezes my shoulder as we walk up to the porch side by side. He smells like metal and freshly cut wood because he's a construction site foreman. It's just his smell. It's one I've always loved and always will love.

"Oh, great. It feels great," I say and mean it.

Mom is waiting on the porch holding the screen door open. "There she is! Our high school senior."

My mom can come off a little flighty with her fly-away, frizzy brown hair, but I know she's really very smart. Dad says she's where my brother and I get our intelligence from.

"Got any plans tonight?" she asks.

"There's an end-of-school party I want to go to."

"Where is it? Who's going? And who are you going with?"

"Eric is picking me up probably around eight, it's at the class president's house, and everybody is going."

I start up the stairs to my room and almost get into a tussle with the hanging quilt on the wall. I might've gotten smart genes from Mom, but I definitely didn't inherit her sense of style. Where she goes for a country-chic look that involves colors like mauve and what I like to call makes-you-want-to-jump-off-a-bridge bluish-gray, I like vibrant colors and sleek, modern design with a hint of whimsy.

"Well, I guess it's okay. Twelve o'clock curfew, though," she calls up to me.

"Okay!"

As soon as the door closes, I bolt over to my closet, stick my hand deep inside the stack of sweaters, and pull out the bag with #400 inside. I have plenty of time to read it again before Eric comes to pick me up.

I spend the next couple of hours or so analyzing every tiny detail. This artist is so talented. His energy signatures—the glowy stuff that appears around a character's hands or eyes just before they use their powers to lay the smackdown on the bad guy—remind me of flame and smoke. And the way he does fabric: so realistic.

Wendy looks especially fabulous in this issue. God, what I wouldn't give to have those knee-high, black and fuchsia boots with the killer stiletto heel.

All too soon, it's time to return the bag and book back to its hiding place and get ready for the party. I take a shower, then pick out a cute summer blouse with ribbon straps I tie into bows on top of my shoulders and a pair of denim shorts. My favorite pair of chunky sandals that also have ribbons as straps, thick white ones, complete the outfit. By the time I've blow-dried my hair, brushed it to a pretty shine, and put on my makeup in a dewy-eyed-princess fashion, I hear the neighbor's dogs barking outside. Eric must be here.

I get my purse and cross my room to go downstairs, but something crunches under my foot before I reach the door. It's the piece of paper with Logan's ominous message and his phone number. It must have fallen out when I opened #400, and I was too engrossed to notice. I get a weird, wiggly feeling in my chest as I stare at the numbers, despite the implication of his words.

"Maddie, Eric is here!" Mom calls from the kitchen after he lays on the horn for a few seconds.

The only place I can think to hide the paper is under my mattress, but what if Mom decides to change the sheets and flip it tonight? She tends to do that kind of stuff when she's waiting for me to get home. One night I came home to find the entire living room rearranged.

If she found it, I'd have to answer all kinds of questions, so I stuff the number in an inside pocket of my purse, telling myself no one will look in there tonight, and go downstairs.

Dad catches me before I dash out the door and pulls out his wallet, but I hold my hand up for him to stop. "I don't need any money."

"Take it anyway, just in case." He hands me a twenty from his tattered, leather wallet and two quarters from his jeans pocket.

"I have a cell phone, you know. Besides, we're not going to be anywhere near a payphone." I hold up the quarters.

"Better to be safe than sorry."

"I always used to put a dime in my shoe when I was your age and going out on the town," Mom says as she walks up and kisses the top of my head.

Out on the town? Oh, boy. "Okay, well, bye y'all." I escape through the front door.

As we pull off my street, Eric revs the engine of his extended-cab truck and peels out, the sound of his screeching tires bouncing off all those quaint little, suburban houses.

"Come on, Eric," I whine. "You think Mom and Dad didn't hear that?"

"Who cares?" he says and pulls out his phone. "Dude, where you at?"

He's probably talking to Peter. They talk on the phone more than Terra and I do, so I just resign myself to another boring ride of listening to boy-talk.

We pass through our normally sleepy college town, but tonight it's alive. Graduating seniors and the new seniors are all over the place, not to mention the college students who are out having one more night of fun before heading home for the summer. It's not a big town, but we do have a Chili's and a Wal-Mart.

We meet up with Terra, Peter, and a bunch of other up-and-coming seniors in an empty parking lot. The air is thick with the smell of exhaust, beer, and juvenile superiority. I must say, it does feel good to be a senior.

Terra and I meet at the back of Eric's truck and immediately go into the elaborate greeting we made up back in ninth grade. It starts with two high fives, then goes into two shoe kicks, one hand heart, a hug, and finishes with a big kiss on the cheek.

"Have you asked your parents yet?" Terra asks.

It takes me a second to remember what I was supposed to have asked them. "Oh, the concert. No, not yet."

"Oh my God, what's wrong with you?"

"I'm sorry, I just forgot."

"Sometimes I wonder whether you actually like Allison." She sighs. "You don't have to, you know."

Oh, but I do have to. My "love" of Allison is part of my image, and I need that image to remain intact. Especially now with the Logan debacle. "No, no. That's not it at all. It's just with the last day of school and—"

"Let's move 'em out!" Eric yells over the crowd, saving me from having to make up yet another lie. Terra is the one part of my double life that feels real, despite everything. I hate lying to her almost as much as I hate what would happen if I didn't.

We're a force to be reckoned with, a parade of cars, trucks, and borrowed parents' minivans, as we drive down the main street of Natchitoches, hooting and hollering out our windows.

This is considered one of those rites of passage in our small town. The new seniors kind of marking their new territory. We pass a cop, and he just honks.

Candy's place is a huge, classic plantation home. Columns line the front, hanging ferns alternating between them. The gravel drive is winding and lined with ancient magnolia trees. We skirt the main house and pull up into the empty field next to it. There are so many vehicles here it looks like the parish fair has come to town early.

Eric gets out and goes to the back of the truck while I touch up my sparkly, pink lip gloss. In the visor mirror, I see him pull out a long, blue bag from the bed of the truck. I hop out and jog to catch up to him, since he's already weaving between the rows of cars.

"What's that?" I ask.

"A tent."

"And what's it for?"

"Sleeping in."

I take a deep, calming breath because he's not being sarcastic. He completely thinks I don't know what a tent is used for. "You planning on sleeping here tonight?"

"I am, you are, everyone is," he says as we make it out of the maze of vehicles and into the empty field. He waves his arm in a broad arc like he's introducing me to the head coach of the New Orleans Saints. Everyone is setting up tents and rolling out sleeping bags. Peter and a few others are hauling wood to the center of the campsite, creating the base of what looks to be the makings of a towering bonfire.

"I can't stay here, I—"

"Just call your parents and tell them you're staying the night with Terra. They'll believe anything you tell them."

Thanks, Eric, for yet another reminder of my spectacular lying ability. "They're expecting me back at midnight, and besides, I hate camping."

"Aw, come on, babe." He drops the tent on a clear spot next to the future bonfire. He wraps his arms around my waist, and lifts me up so we're face to face. "I leave for vacation tomorrow. This could be our last night to really be together."

I can feel my resolve weaken because that is pretty sweet, but the second I let my face soften, he plops me back on the ground and pulls a lighter out of his pocket. Peter tosses him a bottle of lighter fluid. Apparently, they're ready to use profuse amounts of flammable liquid to light the fire.

Two hours later, the ground is littered with cups. Nothing says party like red plastic cups, after all. I've been having a good time. The music is loud and twangy. People I've never spoken to are now good friends of mine, at least for the night. Terra pulls me over to the fire so the squad can do a senior cheer that ends with Rayann Black doing a back-handspring, then puking behind her tent. That's about when I start contemplating how I'm going to get home.

"Where are Candy's parents?" I ask Terra.

"On a beach somewhere. Her older brother is here. He took everyone's keys before they started drinking." She nods at a guy wearing a university sweatshirt, which is currently bunched up around his face because he is upside-down doing a keg stand. And there's Eric right behind him, cheering him on.

"So, everyone's safe, and no one is going nowhere." Instead

of correcting her on her double negative, I just rub my upper arm. Terra is one of those people who likes to emphasize her words with hand gestures, but once she gets a drink or two in her, she becomes one of those people who smack you in the arm to get their point across.

"I cannot wait for the Allison concert. It's going to be so awesome," she says, and on the last smack she misses my arm and glances the side of my boob. "Oh my God, did I just hit your boob? I'm so sor—" She freezes like a coon dog that just heard some rustling in the woods. "Oh my God, I love this song!"

Once Terra skips away to find the source of the music, I find my purse and head toward the vehicles to get some air. I pinball from person to person and finally make it to the improvised parking lot. Only once I'm three rows deep do I let down the tailgate of someone's truck, hop onto it, and look up. The stars are so bright tonight not even the raging fire behind me can dim their glow.

If I were Wendy, a.k.a. The Bright Frenzy, I could just fly home, which would be the most awesome thing ever. Of course, thinking about Wendy brings Logan to mind. The way his eyebrow quirked up in that rascally manner at lunch today…

…and the little slip of receipt paper in my purse.

#5

It had to happen at some point, right? I can't keep #400 forever, as much as I want to, especially since he knows my secret.

I take my cell out and dial his number without looking at the paper because I might have stared at it enough times to memorize it. Before I hit the call button, I go over my options one more time. I don't want to spend the night in a field with a bunch of drunk people—especially not when I'll have to lie to do it. There is no one at this party I would trust to drive me home right now, and I really don't want to call my parents. It would only freak them out and possibly get everyone else in trouble. And even though I know my brother would make the hour drive from Shreveport to pick me up, I don't feel right asking him to do it in the middle of the night.

Plus, I really need to give Logan #400 back.

The downsides are obviously the risk of someone seeing

Logan and me together, and the fact I'm calling a guy I may or may not have a crush on and asking him to pick me up from a party I'm at with my boyfriend.

I tap the green button before I can change my mind.

"Hello?" His voice floats through the phone, all calm and collected. Then, I hear a blood-curdling scream in the background.

"Oh my God, what's going on? Who's screaming?"

"Hold on," he says, and then there's some muffled, scrambling noises. "Dan, turn that down, dude. Blasting the volume is not going to improve your skills."

"Uh, hello?"

"Sorry, the Xbox was too loud." I hear a door shut on his end, and everything gets quiet. "Who is this?"

"I…I have your #400."

"Oh. Well?"

"Well what?" I ask in sort of a snippy tone. Then I remember I'm the one who called him, so I probably shouldn't act snippy.

"Well, what did you think of it?"

"I loved it," I blurt out, then slap a hand over my mouth. Even though I know he knows about me liking comics, it stills feels weird actually admitting it.

"I heard it was good. Did Young One die? Wait, don't tell me."

"Okay, I won't tell you."

"Never mind, tell me. Does he die?"

"Now I'm really not going to tell you." I giggle and tug on a lock of hair. Then, I realize what a fawning girly-girl I'm being and tuck my hand beneath my thigh. "Look, I called because…" I can't finish.

"Because?"

"I kind of need your help," I finally manage.

His tone raises a notch with what sounds like worry. "Are you okay?"

"Oh yeah, I'm fine, I just… I need a ride." I squeeze my eyes shut.

"Sure, where to?"

In the background, I hear the door open. Dan says, "Dude, is that the chick? What does she want? Is it a booty call? It's a booty call, isn't it?"

I shake my head as Logan tells him to go away.

Dan must not listen, because he says, "This can't end well, my friend. What did I say earlier? A hot chick equals high maintenance, which equals you carrying her purse while she shops for shoes."

"Home," I say before Dan can turn him against me. "I need a ride home."

"No problem." More rustling, the *click* of a door shutting, then silence. "Where are you now?"

"Do you know where Candy Southern lives?"

"Yeah, I can be there in fifteen minutes. Is that okay?"

"Perfect. Thank you so much."

"You're welcome, Maddie."

I go through about a million different feelings and thoughts in the few seconds after he hangs up. He knew it was me at the shop. For sure, he knew. Is he going to tell anyone? He hasn't yet, not even Dan, though he must've said *something* because Dan called me a "hot chick" while trying to turn Logan against me. Before I can panic about that, I realize Logan was worried about me. That was sweet. He wanted to know what I thought of the book. He's willing to drive out here for someone he doesn't know.

Also, I really liked the way he said my name.

I run back to tell Terra and Eric I'm heading out. Eric's too busy winning at giant beer pong—seriously, how hard can it be for a quarterback to toss a football into a five gallon bucket?— to really pay attention to me, but Terra wants to know why I'm leaving.

"I'm just tired." That seems to satisfy her because an Allison Blair song comes on and she starts singing it loud enough for everyone to hear.

I go back to my star-gazing spot, stare at the driveway, and try to think of something witty to say when Logan shows up. Nothing comes.

What is *he* going to say? I'm almost positive he's going to laugh at me, at my predicament. I'm a nerd hidden inside a popular girl's body, and the only person that can help me right now is someone I've hardly even acknowledged for fear of social ruin. Man, he must think I'm just a shallow hypocrite.

Why do I want to cry all of a sudden?

Headlights appear on the driveway, and I jog toward them. Logan's beat-up silver Accord pulls into an empty spot, and he leans over to unlock the door. When I open it, a very dim overhead light pops on, and the first thing I see is his smile.

"Hi," I say when I drop into the seat. How witty is that?

"How's it going?" He throws an arm over the back of my seat and turns to watch the back as he reverses.

"Fine." Man, I should write a book. I could call it *Things to*

Say to Ensure You Come Off as an Idiot.

"Good, good." He nods his head.

It's quiet for a minute as we both stare ahead at the road. Finally, I strike on a gem of a conversation starter. "I didn't know you worked at The Phoenix."

"I didn't know you were into comics." He quirks that eyebrow at me. "I haven't seen you in the store before."

"I usually just download my issues."

"Aw, why would you do that when you have a perfectly good comic shop in town?" He taps his fingers against the steering wheel along with the music on the radio.

"I don't know." I shrug. "It's just more convenient, I guess."

"But don't you miss actually holding the paper in your hands?"

"Yeah, I do. I miss the smell, too. There's just something about it."

"Exactly. The old ones especially, before they went to that glossy paper."

This feels so weird, surreal even, to be having a real-life conversation with someone about comics. I catch myself bobbing my head, agreeing with every word he says. I can feel a goofy grin on my lips. I literally have to shake my head, rattle my brain, to come back to my senses.

I keep quiet for the rest of the drive. So does he, but I can feel him flick glances at me which, in turn, causes me to flick glances right back. He's wearing jeans and a black T-shirt. His hair sticks out at weird angles, but for some reason, the whole messy, not-a-care-in-the-world thing makes him seem even more magnetic.

The only noise is the college radio station playing quietly

through the front speakers. A Yoda bobblehead shimmies on the dashboard. The car is clean or, at least, my seat is. It's obvious he tidied up before coming to get me. In other words, the back seat is crammed full of books, CDs, and notebooks. There are a couple of long, white cardboard boxes I know are made for comic book storage. My fingers itch to open them.

When we make it to my house, I see my mom's silhouette through the glass in the front door. She turns the porch light on. It's 11:30. I'm early. She sticks her head out the door, and I wave. Her worried frown is replaced by a relieved smile.

"I'll just run up and get your book," I say.

"Don't worry about it. I'll get it later."

"But aren't you ready to read it?"

"Yeah, but I can wait. You look nice tonight, by the way." He clears his throat. Even in the barely there light, I can see his ears turn red.

Is blushing contagious? Because my cheeks start to burn. "Thanks, and thanks for the ride."

"Any time."

"Okay." There's a second where I forget what it is I'm supposed to do next. Eric usually lunges across the seat and gives me a sloppy kiss, but this isn't a date, and Logan isn't my boyfriend. Or Eric. I tuck my hair behind my ear nervously and look him in the eyes. They are blue, not the color of the ocean blue, not the blue of a morning sky, just pure blue.

Somehow, my mind kick starts, and I remember what the next step is. "Well, good night."

"'Night." He smiles a real smile. This one is so honest and bright it's almost blinding in its cuteness.

His car almost stalls as it pulls out of the driveway. I wonder what he'll do with the rest of his night. Is he going to continue playing video games with Dan? Or is he going to curl up in bed with a stack of comics?

Now I'm thinking about him in bed. Possibly wearing nothing but a pair of Iron Man boxers. I shake my head. I have got to get a hold on myself.

. . .

The next morning, I wake up to the smell of French toast drifting through the house. A weight leaves my shoulders when I realize today is the first official day of summer. I hate the heat—it's easier to get warm than it is to get cool—but the summer has always been my time. I don't have to pretend nearly as much. By the end of this week, I'll probably be completely caught up on my to-be-read pile—or file since it's really just a folder on my computer—which means I'll need to buy a new comic journal because the current one will be full.

But, before I start rolling around in my nerd-world like Scrooge McDuck in a mountain of gold, I need sustenance. When I get downstairs, Mom is at the stove. I stack a couple of pieces of buttery, syrupy goodness on a plate and sit down at the table to dig in.

"Do you know where the air mattress is? Roland is coming home for the weekend soon, and he might need it," Mom says, and my heart fills with happy.

Roland is my older brother who goes to college in Shreveport. He was my hero growing up. Whenever he does come home, we stay up way too late catching up on comic book talk. We're going to have so much to discuss when it comes to The Super Ones. I can't wait to hear his opinion on the significance of The Young One's OCD in comparison to Marcus's drinking problem. And I'll be able to show off another completed comic journal. Ro gave me my first empty one after I spent hours poring over his own towering stack of journals when I was a kid. On one hand, I want to curse him for ever getting me into comics. On the other, I wouldn't have it any other way.

"It's in the hall closet by your room, but I doubt he'll use it. He'll just end up on the couch like always," I say.

"I know, but I want to make him as comfortable as possible. If I have to hear any more psychobabble about why I turned his room into a craft room, I'm going to lose it. Anyway, did you have fun at the party?"

"Yeah, it was okay."

"Whose car was that last night?"

I almost choke on my food because the last thing I need is Mom poking her nose into the situation. She's not exactly the biggest Eric fan, and if she thought I was talking to someone else, I'd never hear the end of it. "Eric wasn't ready to leave so I got a ride with Logan."

Mom sits across the table with a cup of coffee. "Who's Logan?"

"He's just a guy in my class."

"Who are his parents?"

"Mom, come on."

"Okay, sorry, I just like to know who my daughter is friends with."

"We're not friends," I say, then backtrack, thinking she'll want to know why I let a stranger drive me home. "Not really, anyway. We just know each other from school."

Dad comes in through the back door, stomping his boots on the welcome mat to get rid of any dirt. He always has had perfect timing.

"Good morning, Madelyne Jean, Dorothy Ann." He nods at us both like a true gentlemen. "What do you have planned today, Maddie?"

"I thought I'd go over and hang out with Terra. Maybe go swimming."

Mom sighs. "Ah, to be young again. Nothing to do but hang out and go swimming."

I grab my plate and put it in the dishwasher. "It's a tough life, but someone has to live it."

"Don't forget your sunblock!" Mom yells as I dart up the stairs.

When I get to my room, I give Eric a required girlfriend call. There's no answer, of course, so I text him a quick message.

Maddie: *Have a great time! Will miss you :)*

I'm such a horrible person because that is a big, fat lie. Do I wish he'll have a great time? Sure. But will I miss him? Not really.

I put on my swimsuit and cover it with a fitted white T-shirt and some shorts. Then, I grab #400 from my closet and give it one last read through. I'm going to miss it, but I'll have my own copy in another month or two, right? It's not like this one is special or anything because it's Logan's.

I fold the Phoenix bag with perfectly straight creases until it's a nice flat square that will fit in my comic journal. After it's safely put away, I carefully place #400 in my backpack along with some sunblock.

I prop some shades on my head and give myself a once-over in the mirror. There I am, just a normal teenage girl ready to go swimming with her best friend on the first official day of the summer. Looking at me, no one would ever guess I'm really on my way to visit the nerd capital of Natchitoches.

#6

With my jacket on, the hood of it pulled up and over my cap, and my shades firmly in place, I pull into the back parking lot of The Phoenix next to the only other vehicle, Logan's. I dial his number.

"Hey, Maddie," he answers, his smooth voice causing a shiver to float across the back of my neck.

"How did you know it was me?" I look around. Is he hiding in the bushes or something?

"I programmed your number into my phone."

Great. What if someone goes through his contacts and finds me? "Right. Anyway, I have your comic."

"I can't come get it now because I'm at the shop, but maybe later we—"

"I'm parked out back," I say quickly before he can tempt me with what *we* can *maybe* do *later*.

"Well, come on in."

"Could you just come out here?"

There's a long silence before he says, "Fine," and hangs up.

Double great. Now he's mad at me. And why should I care? It's not like we could ever actually be friends. My kind and his kind just don't mix.

The beat-up metal door in front of me slams open, banging against a cinder block probably used to prop it open, and out comes Logan. He stalks to my passenger-side door, shoulders hunched, hands in pockets. The window is open, so he just shoves a hand through it and makes a give-it-here motion with his fingers. As I open my backpack to get the book, I lean over, trying to see his face.

"Sorry I made you come out here. You probably need to watch the store, right?"

"Dan's keeping an eye on things," he says in a flat tone.

"What a good friend."

I pet the #400's cover one last time. Am I stalling? I don't know, but for whatever reason, I don't want him to be mad at me. Thinking it's the best way to get us back into friendly territory, I hand it to him. He snatches it away without so much as a thank you, turns to go back inside, then stops. He leans over and sticks his head through the window, a scowl on his face.

I prepare myself for whatever rant he's about to lay on me, but when he sees me, his face goes blank. His eyes move from my glasses to my hat to my hoodie and back to my face. I'm used to these kinds of blatant appraisals. I'm a cheerleader, for God's sakes. But Logan's stare makes me feel naked. Heat rises in my cheeks. Then he ruins it by laughing long and hard.

"What?" I ask.

"Are you serious?" He wipes away a tear from the corner of his eye. "In the name of all that is good and holy, why are you dressed like that? It's almost a hundred degrees out here."

"I…I get cold."

"You get cold?" he asks, then lets out a sound that can only be interpreted as a scoff.

I hate scoffs.

"Yeah, I get cold."

He shakes his head as he laughs some more. The heat in my cheeks has turned to a scalding burn. This is what I get for allowing someone to peek at *that* side of me. He can just laugh his ass back into that store and out of my perfectly fine life.

I throw the car into reverse. "Enjoy your comic."

"Wait!" he yells, gripping the door handle.

I stop just for a second thinking his shirt or something is caught, but he takes the chance to fling open the door and sit in the passenger seat.

He fastens the seat belt, closes the door, and slaps the top of the car through the open window. "Okay, I'm ready. Where are we going?"

I can't think of a response due to being completely and utterly flabbergasted at his audacity.

"I'm hungry. You hungry? I'll buy."

I glare at him over the top of my sunglasses and purse my lips.

He sighs. "I'm sorry I laughed at you, but please don't go. You want to come inside for a second? Get some water? Cool off?"

"I can't. I have to…" I trail off as I stare at the metal door hanging open. God, what I wouldn't give to go in.

"Come on, just for a minute. You'll kick yourself later if you don't, and you know it. I promise no one will see you. Dan will stay up front for as long as I'm in the back."

"I'm not worried about anyone seeing me."

He raises an eyebrow. "Of course not. You're just trying to start a new fashion trend. I'm sure the creepy-creeper style will take off."

I remove my shades and look between him and the open door. I can see stacks and stacks of those white, cardboard boxes lined up against the wall in there. When will I ever get this chance again?

It's not like I really have anything to do. I chew on my bottom lip a little before giving in. "Just for a minute."

Before I'm even out of my car, he comes around to meet me with that annoying smile plastered across his face.

I glare at him. "Will you stop that?"

"Stop what?"

"Smiling."

"Okay." But he just keeps on smiling and nudges my shoulder with his. How can I stay mad at that? Heaving a sigh, I trudge toward The Phoenix.

The second I cross the threshold, the smell of aged paper hits me, and I breathe deep. I pause and take it all in as Logan closes and locks the door behind us. I feel like I've been given an all-access pass to Disney World. Not only are there tons of boxes, but there's a row of big cardboard cutouts in the corner lined up like they're waiting to buy movie tickets. The walls are covered with gorgeous posters done by some of the best artists ever. There's George Perez's cover of DC's *Infinity Crisis* #7 with Superman cradling Supergirl's torn and battered body. And by the door that leads to the front of the store, is a really long poster of the X-Men team done by Jim Lee. I know it's Jim Lee because the way he does hair and brow furrows is unmistakable.

"Any particular title you want to read?" Logan asks.

"Where's your boss? He wouldn't like me being back here, I bet."

"Actually, I'm kind of my own boss. My parents own The Phoenix. All you see before you will one day be mine." He spreads his arms wide.

Talk about a dream job! I'd never leave. They wouldn't even have to pay me. "That is so awesome." I let my fingers slide over one of the boxes. I can almost hear the thousands of voices inside begging to tell me their stories.

"It's okay, I guess."

"What do you mean 'I guess'? You get to come *here* every day."

"Well, the shop isn't doing so well lately." He leans one shoulder against the wall.

"Oh, sorry. I didn't realize." Now that I think back over the many times I've passed by the store, I can't remember ever seeing more than one or two cars out front at one time. Rather than think about what that meant to the store, I was more concerned about whether the people driving those cars would notice me ogling the displays in the windows.

"Don't worry about it. Things will pick up soon. So let's see. You like The Super Ones so you'd probably like The Midnight

Judge."

"I've already read that series." I wait for his inevitable response of disbelief, but it never comes.

"Great! I mean, the earlier issues were kind of cliché, but when that new writer took over, wow. Just wow. He took it in a whole new direction." He starts shifting boxes, reading the labels as he goes.

"I know, right? Issue #249 almost made my brain explode when he killed that cop on accident, then totally lost it."

He stops in the middle of picking up another box, turns to me, and there's this moment where I feel like I'm being seen for the first time. I can't quite interpret the look on his face. It's kind of like before when his stare made me feel almost naked, except this time his head tilts to the side and the corner of his mouth turns up just a tiny bit. It's like he just caught a glimpse of something fascinating, but he's not sure what it is.

"I thought the same thing." He takes a step toward to me. "That whole story line was revolutionary, in my opinion."

I smile, and he smiles more. The question I've asked myself at least a million times since I first saw Logan pops into my head: What is it about this guy? He's not "movie star" hot. He wears one of those old calculator watches and has a scattering of freckles, for goodness sake. Then, he checks the time on that silly watch, and my stomach goes all wibbley-wobbley. I have to bite my lip to suppress a giggle when I picture him tapping away on that tiny calculator, working out complicated equations. He would have a crease between his eyebrows as he concentrated on the numbers. I would smooth it away with a kiss, and he'd look up at me and…

I put a chokehold on my thoughts before they get any further. No fantasizing about kissing adorable nerd boys for me, no matter how kissable they look. Especially right now.

Suddenly, I realize we've been standing there smiling at each other for way too long. "Oh, and when his best friend is taken and brainwashed into becoming a super assassin and Judge has to kill him, too, only to find out about the brainwashing thing later."

He nods at my rambling and takes a few more steps closer. I step back. Sort of.

"It was so sad when he found out he could have reversed the effects of the brainwashing and saved him," he says in a near whisper. He leans forward and reaches around me to tap the box I'm propped against. "I think that run of issues is in this box."

We're so close now I can feel the leftover heat from the sun as it leaves his clothes and skin. He's wearing a worn gray T-shirt that's kind of tight on his shoulders. He's not buff like Eric, but he's not skin and bones, either.

"Neat." I could smack myself in the forehead for such a lame response. But it's like my brain has given up trying to supply me with intelligent words and has switched to "grin like a fool" mode.

"We could, uh—"

He stops midsentence, glances down at me, and swallows hard. When his lips part, I get the same light-headed feeling I do when I complete a triple back handspring. His fingertips whisper across my forearm, and my eyes close. The low hum of cars passing by outside seems to calm my rapid heartbeat. My hand reaches for him without my permission, no matter how wrong

I know hooking my finger into his jeans pocket will be. Logan leans closer, like he knows what I'm about to do, and I'm pretty sure I'll never be able to breathe again when I open my eyes and see how he's looking at me.

And wouldn't you know it, that's the moment Dan realizes he has no idea how to run a cash register.

"Dude!" he yells from the front of the store. "How do I get this S-O-B to open again?"

Logan clears his throat and steps back. "I'll be right back."

When he leaves, I fan my face, then lay both palms on my warm cheeks. Well, that didn't take long. I haven't even been here a full five minutes, and I almost mauled him.

What's wrong with me? One second, I'm concerned about whether or not someone will see my name in his phone contacts, and the next, I want to strangle Dan for interrupting what could have been the hottest, nerd-boy kiss of my life. I have a *boyfriend*. A boyfriend who wouldn't like me kissing another guy. Probably.

Logan's voice drifts through the door from the front counter. "What did you do to it?"

"I didn't do anything. It hates me, that's all," Dan says, and then it sounds like he slams his fist on the buttons. The register makes a lot of dinging sounds, and then there's a strange noise like *whurrrrr, tick, tick.*

I might be here for a while.

• • •

I end up on the floor surrounded by comic books, having opened the nearest box and rifled through it. I could seriously live here. All I would need is some water and maybe some of that dehydrated astronaut food.

I suddenly get the feeling I'm being watched and look up. Logan is leaning against the frame of the open door.

"Looks like you're having fun."

"Is this okay? I promise I'll put them back in order."

He laughs. "It's fine." He reaches up and turns a little white knob on a panel by the door. Music starts playing from an ancient speaker in the corner. The sound quality is kind of crackly, but I like it. The whole atmosphere seems to meld together into a piece of my own personal heaven. Vintage comics, music that hasn't been autotuned to hell and back, and another person who likes all the same things to share it with? It doesn't get better than this.

I realize the music isn't coming from a CD but from a radio station when the deejay announces the next song.

"Keep listening, all you wonderful people stuck here for the summer. You're lucky I'm one of you." A kind of reggae song starts.

"Is that the college station?" I ask.

He plops down on the other side of my increasing wall of books. "Yeah. You listen to it?"

"Not really. You were listening to it last night in the car."

"Oh, right. I have my own show this summer so I'm trying to make sure I don't copy any of the other personalities." He shrugs like it's no big deal, but I can tell he's proud of the fact.

"Wow, cool. Did you have to apply to NU for that?" I pull out another comic as casually as possible, but I really want to bury my face in it.

"Kind of. I wanted to get started as soon as possible in the business so I went to the professor who's in charge of the station and asked if I could help out over the summer. He gave me my own show. Figured I might be able to drum up interest from the high school kids. I doubt that will actually happen, but I didn't want to tell him that."

"Why don't you think that'll work?"

He shakes his head. "People don't listen to the radio anymore. It's all digital downloads, iTunes, and YouTube. Besides, it's not like I have a loyal fan-base or anything."

"I'm sure it'll be awesome. When's your show on? I'll listen— it's the least I can do."

"It's a nightly show from seven to nine."

"That's a good time spot, right?"

"Yeah, one of the best, actually. I have no idea why he let me have it."

I watch his every move now. He stacks and unstacks the comics. He studies one cover, then moves onto another, trying his best not to glance at me. I know that's what he's doing because every time he looks up and I'm looking at him, his eyes dart back down. It gets quiet, so I go back to my book.

We spend the next few hours thumbing through different issues. He'll show me a particular series of panels that are well done. I'll show him a classic ad for Sea-Monkeys or x-ray glasses. We have a couple of conversations about the importance of this character or that event. He checks on Dan every once in a while, which always ends with Dan saying something like, "What the hell are you doing back there anyway?" or, "Dude, you know I'm not getting paid for this shit, which is probably against the law.

Child labor going on right here in the heartland of America!"

"Is he really that upset? I can go if you need to be up there," I say after the third time Logan comes back from up front.

"He's fine. He doesn't do anything else but hang out here anyway. Plus, I let him read all the books he wants when he watches the register."

Just then, my phone goes off. My ringtone is a song about this guy who wishes he would have said something to this girl he has great chemistry with. I love how the singer sounds like he's speaking from the heart.

I jump up when I see it's Eric calling.

"I should…" I glance from the screen of my phone to Logan. His brow is furrowed.

For a moment, I contemplate not answering. It's hard to let go of this place, but Eric is considerate even if he isn't the smartest dog in the hunt. He might call my parents and say he can't get in touch with me. Then they might call Terra, who wouldn't know anything about going swimming today. I'll be in super-duper trouble before the summer even gets started.

I put one hand over my other ear to block out the grainy music. "Hello."

"Hey, babe, sorry I didn't answer this morning. Where did you go last night?"

"I, uh, just wanted to get home. I was tired. Just wanted to sleep in my own bed."

"How'd you get home?"

I cut my gaze to Logan and catch him staring. He quickly becomes immersed in another cover. "My brother was in town. I just called him."

There's some yelling in the background, and Eric says, "All right, dude, I'm coming! I have to go, babe. I'll talk to you later, okay?"

"Okay, bye."

"Was that the quarterback boyfriend?" Logan asks when I hang up, not even looking at me.

"Yeah, he's on vacation in Florida."

"Must be nice." He finally looks at me and crosses his arms. "So, I'm your brother, huh?"

All that camaraderie and all the awesome comic and radio talk…gone, as all the comfortable leaves the situation

"He can get jealous." I start putting the books back into their boxes because it is definitely time to go.

"Just leave them. I'll get it."

And now I've hurt his feelings. Great going, me. I gather my things and remind myself how bad of an idea this was. I really shouldn't be jerking this guy around. He doesn't deserve my brand of crazy messing up his life.

"Well, thanks for all of…this. I'll see you around, maybe," I say before unlocking the door and stepping out into the boiling heat.

I swear he says something under his breath behind me. Something that sounds like, "Yeah, right."

Man, I suck at life.

#7

That evening, after hamburgers, Tater Tots, and Brussels sprouts—Mom lives by the "something green with every meal" rule—I watch a couple of shows with Dad. There's a teen drama on I would normally be watching at this time, but the only reason I watch the show is so I can keep up when Terra and the other girls talk about it. But since it's summer and Dad's home, we're watching reruns of a science fiction show.

For the record, sci-fi is infinitely more dramatic than those prime-time soap operas. So what, your boyfriend's dad is having an affair with your mom? That's nothing compared to a love triangle between two guys and a girl in the middle of outer space while there's a psycho bounty hunter hiding somewhere on their ship. Why they ever canceled this show is beyond me.

When one of the two guys dies valiantly by sacrificing himself for the other guy and the bounty hunter is finally sucked out into the void, I stand to head to my room.

"We still having our anime marathon tomorrow night?" Dad calls after me.

"You know it. I can't wait to see Akira."

There's another reason summer rocks: our marathons. Last year we did Hitchcock, *Battlestar Galactica*, and Clint Eastwood films.

In my room, I turn the radio on to 91.5, The Devil. Just as I'm propping myself up on my bed with my laptop, Logan's show starts.

"Welcome to the very first broadcast of Logan's Show of Awesome," he says, and I giggle. I can't believe it, but his voice sounds even better coming through my speakers. There's just nothing to compare it to. It is what it is: delicious.

"You're in for a treat, people. Logan, that's me, will be on every night this summer from seven to nine, bringing you the most spectacular, mind-blowing fantasticness you've ever heard. And I want you to share your fantasticness with me. So give me a call." When he rattles off the number, I program it into my phone.

"To get things going, here's a song that's been stuck in my head all day."

Familiar hard strumming of a guitar begins. I reach for my phone out of habit, but it's not ringing. My mouth drops open, and I stare at the stereo.

Yep, that's my ringtone, the first song played on Logan's Show of Awesome. I'm full-on smiling by the end of it.

"All right, let's see if we have a caller with some awesomeness to share. Ben? What? Oh, no callers yet. Well, that's okay, they're probably just stunned by the amazingness of that last song." He sounded sad when he asked Ben, whoever that is, about callers.

Maybe I should call in. I could disguise my voice like I did the other day at The Phoenix. But that's a stupid idea. I wasn't fooling anyone then, and I wouldn't fool anyone now. And just me calling in isn't going to fix much. One caller does not a hit show make.

No, I have a much better idea.

I turn on my laptop as the next song begins. I've never heard this one, but I'm liking it. I pull up every social network I'm on. There are about five, all with the same group of friends except one I call my nerd circle. It's made up of people across the country who aren't scaredy cats about expressing their love of all things geeky like I am.

On each site I post the same message:

Just stumbled across the most awesome radio show on the local college station. Turn to 91.5 NOW! Sooo cool!

This is the perfect way to return the favor Logan did for me without him knowing it and without anyone finding out about my little secret. I just hope it works.

And it does. By the middle of the show, Logan is bantering back and forth with callers.

"Wow, a shoe sale at the mall in Alexandria? Fifty percent off! I don't know who Jimmy Choo is, but he sounds amazing, Megan."

"I don't watch *To Be a Teenager*, but that episode sounds nuts, Melissa. I'll have to start DVRing it." And on and on he went.

Mostly, the callers are girls my age, which makes sense

because they're the majority of my friends on those websites.

"Can I get your real phone number?" a girl named Capri asks, and I frown at the radio. That was a little forward. And who names their kid after a pair of pants? Might as well just call her "Stirrup" or "Bootcut."

"Oh, I... That's nice of you to ask, but I shouldn't give it out over the air," Logan says.

"I can wait for commer—" Capri's voice cuts off.

"Oops, looks like we lost you, Capri, sorry. Anyway, here's another song."

I laugh like a cartoon villain at that as I check my posts again. Everyone's commenting with stuff like, "I love this song he's playing right now!" and, "He sounds so cute!"

I've done a good deed...I think.

My phone rings for real this time. It's Terra, and I know what she wants—an update on the Allison Blair concert. There's still ten minutes left of Logan's show, so I mute my phone, feeling like a horrible person for not answering.

"Well, that's the end of the show, everybody. And what a great one it was, too. I have to tell you I've had pretty much the best day ever, and I have a feeling someone out there helped make it that way. She probably doesn't want me to say her name on air, but I am going to say thanks. Thanks, Wonderful Wendy."

My stomach flutters. He has to be talking about me. Wonderful Wendy was the name of a five-issue storyline in The Super Ones where The Bright Frenzy was introduced. He knows I'll get the reference.

I almost jump off my bed and hug the stereo.

"And on that note, we'll end the show just as we began it."

My song starts again, and I flop back on my bed, breathless. This is one of those moments you live life for, I'm sure of it.

. . .

The next day, I give Terra a call because things just feel weird since we didn't have our nightly phone call last night. I feel like I've betrayed the Soul-Sisters. This is unacceptable.

"Hey, where were you last night?" she asks right off the bat.

"Huh? Oh, that's right. I saw you called after I got out of the shower, but I was so tired I went right to bed. Mom forced me to help her in the garden most of the day. Do you realize how much water it takes to make things grow? It's ridiculous. Anyway, how much are tickets for the Allison concert?" I know anytime the A-word is mentioned, all other thoughts leave Terra's head.

"Depends on the seats. I've been looking at the floor plan, and the ones I really want are a couple hundred dollars, but the fifty dollar seats are okay. Why? Did you ask them?"

"I'm about to. I just wanted to have all my facts straight."

"Oh my God, I hope they say yes. Rayann's parents said yes, but I don't want to go without you."

Awwww. The girl has such a big heart. The first time we met was in ninth grade biology. We had this really old teacher, Mr. McCoy, who was basically bug-nuts crazy. He was really passionate about biology, but his hearing wasn't great so he'd mumble. A lot. Plus, he'd hop from subject to subject every class, trying to shove as much knowledge into our young, malleable brains as possible. Photosynthesis to osmosis to cell structure to the Genome Project, all in one class period. It was seriously confusing. By the third day of class, most of the students had given up on even attempting to take notes. I, on the other hand, was determined to write down every topic Mr. McCoy touched on because if I got straight As, I could try out for the cheerleading squad.

Terra and I were seated next to each other. One day, she struck up a conversation with me about crazy Mr. McCoy, and we decided to band together. We made a great team, too. When old McCoy would start moving too fast, I'd nudge Terra's foot, and she'd distract him. Sometimes she'd ask him a question pertaining to what he was supposed to be talking about. Sometimes she'd just point out the window and yell something like, "Mr. McCoy, isn't that one of those super-rare butterflies that eats its young?" This would give me plenty of time to catch up on my notes. Then, he'd always ask, "Now where was I?" and I could always make him pick up with whatever I wanted him to. By the end of the second week of school, Terra and I were inseparable.

If I could ever build up the guts to tell anyone about my little secret, she'd be the first person I'd go to, but that'll never happen because there is no way I'd risk losing her. At first, I saw her as my ticket to popularity. Pretty shallow, I know. But now... life would seriously suck without her goofy hand talking and unparalleled knowledge of everything Allison Blair.

So, I guess that's why, after getting off the phone with Terra, I go directly to Mom and Dad to ask if I can go to the Allison Blair concert and come back to my room with fifty dollars in my pocket.

• • •

During the next few days, I develop a routine: wake up, kill time, listen to Logan's Show of Awesome, go to bed. It's a pretty boring existence, I know, but things start to get interesting when, on his Monday night show, Logan throws down the gauntlet.

"Before I say good night, there's one last thing I need to send out into the universe, folks," he says, his voice echoing through my bedroom. "To Wonderful Wendy, I hope you're listening, because tomorrow I'll be you-know-where with something I think your #400 heart won't be able to resist."

He's completely and totally right, of course. There's no way I can resist.

#8

Me: *I'm here.*
Awesome Logan: *I don't see you. Where are you?*
Me: *In the back.*
Awesome Logan: *You have to come in the front door. No hat, no shades.*
Me: *Why?*
Awesome Logan: *Those are the rules.*

I toss my phone in my purse and slam my fist against the steering wheel. Then, I shake my hand because that hurt.

"I will not let him get to me," I say out loud to the interior of my car, but saying it does not make it so. He certainly got to me the other day with his comic book talk and cute watch. I'm convinced I'll never be able to smell that old book smell and not think of him. Which is *not* good because I have a boyfriend.

Straight ahead is the backdoor to The Phoenix, and no matter how hard I try to use my imaginary mind powers to get Logan to walk through it, it's not moving.

He's really going to make me go through the front sans disguise? What could he possibly have for me that's worth exposing my nerd tendencies to the populace of Natchitoches?

I won't do it. I won't fall for it. He can't manipulate me like this.

Maybe if I run, I can make it inside before anyone sees me.

He better not be standing there with a box of chocolates and a teddy bear.

I take off my Celtics cap, shades, and hoodie and clutch my purse to my chest with one hand. The other hand rests on the door handle. I take a deep breath and start counting in my head.

One... Two... Three!

I'm out of the car and down the alley between The Phoenix and Mes Amis in seconds. In front of the store, there's a car in the parking lot. Crap! I shove the front door open so hard the bell overhead clangs like I offended its mother and run at full speed down the middle aisle.

The next events seem to happen in slow motion, like I have the super-ability to stop time. Logan steps out at the end of the aisle, blocking my way to the back, his eyes wide and mouth hanging open. He puts his hands up to get me to stop. I try to put on the brakes, but it's too late. We collide, his arms wrap around me as we fall, and our foreheads bang together. My head spins a little as we lay on the floor in a tangled heap, me on top of him.

The moment I get a fraction of my wits back, I brace my hands on the floor on either side of his chest, but when I try to push off, his hold tightens, keeping me firmly in place.

"Are you all right?" His mouth is so close to my ear his breath tickles it when he speaks.

"I'm fine," is all I can say as I recover from the goose bumps tripping down my arms. "Are *you* okay?"

When we landed, it felt like he banged his head pretty hard on the not-so-soft floor. My fingers go to the back of his head as I pray I didn't give the poor guy a concussion. At my touch, he turns his head even more, so his nose and lips are against my jaw. The goose bumps on my arms seem to forget I was trying to recover from them and redouble their efforts.

"Yeah," he says on a breath, his arms tightening around me. "I'm okay. One could even say I'm euphoric. Ecstatic. Floating on cloud nine, even."

My brain has gone into full-blown "grin like a fool" mode again. I pull back a little and turn to him. I feel my way over his scalp, searching for a bump, and he hits me with the brightest smile I've ever seen.

That's when my brain just gives up and turns to mush.

Satisfied he isn't concussed because no one in pain could pull off a smile that flirty, I push up again. This time he lets me. And, here I am, straddling a hot guy in the middle of a comic shop. The apples of his cheeks turn an endearing pink, and his hands drop to my waist.

"Ahem," a voice says from above us. "I believe you dropped this, m'lady."

The spell between Logan and me breaks, and I look up. Dan is standing there, holding my purse out to me. His brows knit together, and I think he mouths the words, "No way."

Logan and I untangle and stand. I take my purse from Dan, curtseying slightly. Isn't that the proper response when someone calls you "m'lady?"

"Thanks." I try hard not to look either of them in the eye.

"Dude, I told you to stay in the back," Logan says in a low whisper.

Dan drags his eyes from me to glare at Logan. "Well, excuse the hell out of me for trying to help. I heard a crash and thought someone was hurt. You could've fallen. On a pair of scissors. Slit your jugular. How was I to know? Next time you're in need of life-saving action, don't come crying to me," he says, then his voice mimics a whiny child. "'Dan, help me, I've broken my spleen,' because you know what I'm going to say? 'Sorry about the spleen, dude, I have to stay in the back room for all of eternity.'" He finishes his tirade and crosses his arms.

Logan shakes his head and turns to me. "He can exaggerate sometimes."

"Me? Exaggerate? That's a crock of—"

Logan interrupts. "Dan, this is Maddie. You know her, right? She goes to our school?" He raises his eyebrows and stares at his friend.

"Dude, of course I know who Maddie Summers is, I'm not oblivious." He turns to me and in a low voice—or as low a voice as poor Dan can accomplish—says, "How you doin'?"

Before I can respond, Logan grabs Dan by the shoulders and whips him around. "Okay, Dan, thanks for your help. I just need a minute, okay?"

"But I—"

"Good-bye." Logan shoves him toward the back room.

"Geez, fine, I'm going!" Dan says and goes through the open door. But he sticks his head back out. "But you got some 'splainin' to do!" He ducks back before Logan's foot can tag his shin.

"Sorry," Logan says and rubs the back of his neck. Now, not only are his cheeks pink, but so are his ears.

"It's okay. I'm sorry I tackled you. I've watched too many football games, I guess." The moment I mention football, it feels like a weight settles over us. I hurry to change the subject. "So, what is this thing you have for me?"

"You'll see. You want a cup of coffee or a soda or something? I have a break room kind of thing over here." He nods toward the side of the store.

"A soda sounds great."

We go into what is more like a very cramped office than a break room. A built-in corner desk is overflowing with papers and notebooks. Above the desk is a shelf packed full of random action figures, and I find myself gravitating toward it. A short counter on the wall across from the desk holds a coffee maker, a microwave, and a sink. The mini refrigerator sits on the floor by the door, covered in stickers.

I pick up Wendy's action figure and marvel at the craftsmanship. It's fully poseable, and her plastic cape sticks out behind her like she's perpetually standing in front of a wind machine. I pose her with one hand on her hip and one arm stretching above her. I bend one leg slightly at the knee and point her toes. Classic flying pose.

Logan places a cold soda can against the bare skin of my arm, and I jump. "Those are awesome, huh?"

"Yeeees." I draw the word out to emphasize just how

awesome I think they are.

"Speaking of awesome, my radio show is doing really well." He pops the top off my drink and hands it to me.

I stick the can to my lips and start chugging. Maybe he won't prod me if I play the can't-talk-too-busy-hydrating game. "Mmm-hmm?"

"We started off slow the first night, but midway through the show, calls were pouring in. We were so amazed Ben started asking how they heard of the show. As you can imagine, their answers were pretty consistent."

I can't swallow another drop of soda by this point because the carbonation is burning my throat.

"Oh really? Well…" I trail off as I feel bubbling at the base of my throat. This is not good.

Before I can stop myself, I let out the biggest burp I've ever, ever, ever had. I slap a hand over my mouth and stare at Logan whose eyebrows have reached astronomical heights.

"Dude! So not smooth, man! Girls cannot stand rudeness," Dan yells from the back room.

There's a few moments of stunned silence before Logan and I both burst into laughter. He has the best laugh, by the way. It's unabashedly loud, just like my dad's.

The bell over the front door rings, and Logan goes to take care of the customer. In the meantime, I drop into the spinning chair at the desk and position Wendy like she's hanging off my soda can. Terra texts me about what I'm going to wear to the concert, but I don't answer. When I'm in The Phoenix, I feel like I've been sucked into one of Baron Gravity's black holes, a very geeky black hole I don't want to escape from.

Logan comes back and hops up onto the counter. "Anyway, I have something I think you'll like. Think of it as repayment for what you did for my show."

I smile up at him. "I have no idea what you're talking about, but how can I refuse a gift?"

He reaches into his back pocket and pulls out two cards with purple lanyards attached. He holds one out to me. I take it and recognize the logo of Shreveport's NerdCon. In bold, purple font below the speech bubble that holds the letters S.N.C., it reads: V.I.P. DAY PASS.

"Oh my God, how did you get these?" I say, still staring at the pass.

"The S.N.C. sometimes gives out these passes to the businesses in the area that sell comics and stuff, but there is only one comic shop in Shreveport so they sent us a few, too, since we're close. It's only for Saturday," he says quickly, "but it'll still be pretty awesome because all the best stuff happens on Saturday. There's The Super Ones panel. I heard they have some big announcement. And the cosplay contest. All the heavy hitters, like Stan Lee, do their signings that night, too."

If I go and someone finds out, my cover would be blown. Going to S.N.C. would be like shouting from the rooftops I'm a proper geek. That I'm so much of a nerd I want to go and hang out with a coliseum full of them.

But the more I think about it, the more I realize nobody *would* know. I mean, the only people at my school I can think of that might show up are the role-playing guys from the band room, and there's no way they'd pay any attention to me with a bunch of Princess Leias in gold bikinis walking around. Maybe it'd be safer than I think?

I must have been quiet for a while because Logan asks, "Are you okay? You don't have to go. I just thought you'd like it."

"No, I do want to go, I just…" In another life, I would explain everything to him. I would lay all my messed up fears on the line so he could see I'm not worth all these sweet things he's doing for me. But this is not an alternate reality. "I'm just so excited!"

"Really? I didn't think you'd be so easy to convince with your phobia and all. But the thing is, there probably won't be anyone you know there so — "

"Phobia? I don't have a phobia."

"Okay, maybe phobia is the wrong word. It's more like a secret, right?"

"No." I laugh nervously. How do I explain this to him without coming off as a jerk? I could say, "I just don't want to be seen by my friends doing anything incredibly geeky, that's all. I have a reputation to uphold," but for some reason, I don't think that would go over well.

Instead, I go with, "I don't know what you're talking about."

"Oh, that's right, everyone disguises themselves before they enter a store. Everyone lies to their boyfriend about who drove them home when he was too much of an ass to do it himself." He hops off the counter and stands straight as a board, arms crossed.

My mouth opens and closes a few times as I try to come up with some type of response. I've got nothing. It's all true.

"You know what, forget it. I'm sure Dan will be happy to go with me." He tries to take the pass from me, but I tighten my grip.

"Hell, yeah, I'll be happy to go!" Dan yells from the back room, which makes me jerk harder on the pass.

We're in a tug-o-war now. Back and forth we go until I finally stand up and give it all my might.

"No!" I yank one more time, and he releases his hold. I clutch the pass to my chest. "I'm going. I want to go. I want to go because it'll be fun and there'll be lots of people in costumes and… I'm going, okay?"

Logan just stares at me with this blank look on his face for the longest time. I can't tell what he's thinking. I can guess, though. He's probably thinking he underestimated my nutso factor. He's probably wondering what he's gotten himself into.

Finally, his face brightens, and he smiles. "Good. I think it'll be fun, too."

"Damn it!" Dan yells, and I picture him shaking his fist at the ceiling.

#9

The next day, I go back to The Phoenix because (1) I don't think I can handle even looking at Terra right now because I ignored her last five texts about the Allison concert, plus I can't stop thinking about going to NerdCon and what if I get a goofy grin while daydreaming and she asks about it and I have to lie to her? (2) I have nothing else to do but wait for Logan's Show of Awesome to come on. And (3) I just can't help myself.

I still park in the back, but I take my time entering through the front door since there are no cars out front. I stroll up to the counter and wait for Logan's usual greeting.

"Welcome to The Phoenix, anything I can help you with?" He looks up, and a tingle runs down my spine when his expression goes from bored to what I interpret as, "Hey, it's you!"

He closes the comic he was reading. "What are you doing here?"

I hop onto the counter, facing the shelves, and he comes around to stand in front of me. Swinging my legs, I say, "I don't know. I was bored." I shrug. I preen. I even bat my eyelashes.

I shouldn't be doing any of these things, but I can't help it.

"Logan?" a woman's voice calls from the office. I jump down and turn toward the voice, fighting a sudden urge to duck down one of the aisles and out of sight.

The woman pokes her head out of the office. She starts to say something, but when she sees me, she stops.

"This is Maddie, Mom. Maddie this is my mother, Martha," Logan says.

I take a step back, but Logan notices. He lays a staying hand on the base of my back.

"Hi." I wave enthusiastically. Wave? Really? What am I, trying to be rescued from a deserted island or something?

"Hello, Maddie." She steps out of the office and up to the counter. "Do you two go to school together?" She points from me to Logan, back and forth, back and forth. The side of her mouth turns up in a type of smile I recognize immediately, and she props her chin on her fist.

"Yeah," Logan says. "Maddie is a cheerleader. She was also in my English class."

"A cheerleader, huh? I used to cheer at my high school, and in college, too. I was a lot more flexible in those days, but I bet I can remember one of our favorite chants."

Okay, this is kind of a shocker. A high school and college cheerleader goes on to marry a comic shop owner. How did that happen?

She swishes her long brown ponytail behind her back, steps

out into the open aisle, and smoothes down her flowing tie-dyed skirt. She starts clapping in a pretty decent rhythm, nodding her head on each beat, but Logan cuts her off.

"Mom! I was wondering, since you're going to be here all day, could I have the day off?"

Martha stops and looks at Logan, then me. "Sure, honey. Go have fun." She hugs Logan, and to my surprise, she hugs me, too. "If you're going by the house, could you check on Leeloo for me? You know how your dad always forgets to refill the water bowl," she says as she goes back to the office.

Logan stuffs his hands in his pockets. "So, you want to check on Leeloo with me?" His head is tilted down so when he looks at me, waiting for my answer, it's through his lashes. How can I say no to that?

"Sure."

"Great, I'll drive."

We go through the back room, and the smell of it makes me feel all warm and fuzzy. Out back, I get my shades from my car, and when I turn around, Logan is leaning against his hood playing with his keys.

"Can't risk being seen with me?" he says when I put on my shades.

"No, it's sunny. They protect my eyes from harmful UV rays."

"Oh, right." He blushes.

Just like my car, Logan's air conditioner is busted so we drive down College Avenue with the windows rolled down. I look over at Logan and he's nodding his head to the music on the radio. His hair stirs in the wind. No hair products for this guy.

The Natchitoches University campus sprawls out to my right.

Crepe myrtles and azaleas are in bloom, so it's dotted with bright shocks of pink and white.

"Great show last night." I have to yell over the breeze and the music.

"Thanks."

"That Capri girl sure does have a thing for you." Last night, she called in again and again, asking questions about who Wonderful Wendy was and where was you-know-where.

"No, she doesn't. She has a thing for Awesome Logan."

I just laugh and turn my face to the wind, eyes closed, letting the breeze cool the sweat on my forehead.

Even with my eyes closed, I know when we make it to Front Street. The muddy smell of the Cane River hits me, and the car feels like it's going over a million tiny speed bumps. The street has been paved with bricks for a long, long time. Like, before-indoor-plumbing long time. The city replaced the bricks a few years ago and found all kinds of things buried beneath the surface: old tools, pottery, and even a cow skeleton. The street runs straight for four or five blocks and is the main attraction in Natchitoches. The river is on one side of it, and quaint local stores sell everything from books to toys to pastries to instruments on the other side. The whole scene is especially pretty during December when they light up the buildings with twinkling Christmas lights that reflect off the water like drowned fireworks.

The road smoothes out into normal black-top, and eventually Logan turns into a driveway. His house isn't huge but a decent size, and it's nestled in what feels like a rain forest. Martha really loves to landscape, apparently. Ivy has overtaken the fences, the brick walkway from the sidewalk to the front door is lined with freshly planted pansies, and when we pull up under a car cover, the perfumey smell of sweet olive blooms permeate the air.

Logan turns down the radio and looks at me with a very serious expression. "What you are about to witness in no way reflects my own sensibilities. I just wanted you to know that."

"What am I about to witness?"

"It cannot be put into words."

We park, and I follow him to the back of the house. The fenced-in backyard is littered with plastic toys and tricycles, all bleached by the sun. A well-loved swing set sits in the corner. When we get to the door, there's a big gray rock in the middle of the welcome mat.

"Locked out again, Leeloo?" Logan bends down to pet the rock. It turns and snorts, and I realize it's not a rock at all, but a very fat pug. It's face is all smooshed in except for its eyes, which bulge. It catches sight of me and starts making weird honking noises that make me take a step back. Its pink tongue lolls out as Logan rubs its ears. It definitely has the "so ugly it's cute" thing going for it.

Logan opens the door and lets Leeloo half trot, half waddle her way in. He takes a deep breath before following the dog. In a low voice he says, "Here we go."

#10

There's a staircase to my right that leads up to the second floor. Ahead of me is the kitchen where a man sits in front of a laptop at the dining table. He's surrounded by stacks of papers and folders.

"Hey, Dad," Logan says and looks around like he's expecting gremlins to jump out at him.

"Hey, bud. What're you doing home? Thought you were at the store today," his dad says without looking up from the computer. He's a burly, balding guy with glasses and a mustache.

"Mom let me have the day off. Dad, this is—" Logan stops when the ceiling above us rattles like someone just dropped a bowling ball. Screams and giggles echo down the staircase.

Logan's dad stares at the ceiling and yells, "What was that? What's going on up there?"

A high-pitched child's voice answers, "We're okay!"

There's another scream, and the ceiling thumps again. The thumps move to the stairs. A little girl flies down them, followed by another girl who's at least a few years older. A boy who looks to be about twelve is last. They zoom past us and head directly for Logan's dad.

"Daddy, I was just trying to play sparkle ponies, and Jonah said I couldn't—"

"I didn't do anything. She was bugging me about her stupid hairbrush for her stupid horses and—"

"They're not stupid!"

"I tried to tell them you were trying to work, Daddy, but they wouldn't listen, then Jonah jumped off his bed—"

"I did not jump on my bed, I—"

"I didn't say 'on,' I said 'off.' Gah, Jonah, you never listen to anything anyone—"

"—so then he took Miss Pinkstar and started swinging her around by her hair, and I said—"

Logan's dad raises his hands, and there's instant quiet. "Jonah, don't mistreat other people's things. Go back to your room and continue doing whatever it was you were doing. Also, try not to jump *off* your bed so hard."

The boy, Jonah, turns to go back upstairs, grumbling the whole way. He has the same scattering of freckles as Logan.

Logan's dad continues, "Vera, please help your sister find her sparkle pony hairbrush and, Moira, don't scream inside, baby. We use our inside voices when we're in the house, right?"

"Okay, Daddy," the littlest, who is Moira, answers and goes back up the stairs. She's wearing the most adorable polka-dotted sundress I've ever seen.

Vera goes to follow her sister but stops when she notices me. "Hi, I'm Vera. You want to play Candyland?"

"She doesn't want to play Candyland. Go help Moira," Logan says as he ruffles Vera's curly, blond hair.

Vera bats at Logan's hand and says, "Okay, I'll go find Candyland," then darts upstairs.

"Sorry you had to see that," Logan says in a whisper.

"I actually really like Candyland," I say.

Logan rolls his eyes before turning back to his dad who is already immersed in the laptop screen again. "Dad, this is Maddie. Maddie, this is my dad, Steve. Have you filled Leeloo's water bowl today?"

"Hi, Maddie, and yes, I have. Your mother put you up to this, didn't she? I swear, I forget one time, and it's like I'm completely neglecting the dog forevermore."

"No, she didn't put me up to it." Logan grins as he motions for me to follow him. "Want to hang out for a bit?"

"Sure." I'm dying to see his room. What kinds of nerd treasures await?

At the top of the stairs, we go right, in the opposite direction of the tiny voices. As we walk down the hall, I glance into a couple of random rooms. What the house lacks in size, it makes up for in comfort. One room is pink, pink, pink. The bed is a four-poster with a frilly canopy. What a lucky little girl. In another room, Jonah sits at a desk with Legos. Whatever he's building, it's massive. Logan leads me to a room at the end of the hall.

He pushes the door open. "I just want to get a couple of things, and then we can go."

We walk into what must be his room. The walls are painted

a sky blue. Various movie and video game posters are tacked up. More action figures are scattered on his nightstand and computer desk. His bed is made, but there's a pile of dirty clothes hidden behind the open door. I wish I could decorate my room exactly like this, except for the poster of a busty Lara Croft.

At the bookshelf, he tilts his head to read the spines.

"Can I ask you something?" I've been dying to ask him this question ever since my first excursion into The Phoenix.

He pulls a book off the shelf. "Sure."

"How did you know it was me? The other day?"

His blue, blue eyes travel from my toes to my forehead. I start to feel a little fidgety under his stare, so I sit down on the bed.

He comes over and sits next to me. Our thighs touch, and it takes all my effort not to lean against him. My heart feels like it's knocking on my rib cage.

In the ten months I've been dating Eric, I can't remember ever feeling this way. Not when he kissed me, not when he gave me flowers for Valentine's Day, not even when he wore a tux for prom.

Right now, I feel like if I don't touch Logan's freckles or wrap my pinky finger around his, I'm going to spontaneously combust.

"Your hair," he says eventually, and my hand automatically goes to tuck it behind my ear, but it's in a ponytail so there's nothing to tuck.

"My hair?"

"Among other…things. Your voice, the way you purse your lips when you're concentrating. I sit two seats back and one row over from you in English. I see a lot of that ponytail."

"Oh." I pause as the gears turn in my head. "Is that why you pretended to see something behind me?"

He nods. "I was pretty sure, but I had to see your hair to be positive."

He smiles, and we both just sit there for a second, staring and smiling, until a little voice says from the open door, "Are you guys going to kiss?"

We both jump. Logan sort of coughs before getting up to close the door. "Good-bye, Vera." When he turns around, *awkward* isn't a strong enough word to describe how I feel.

Desperate for a distraction, I point to the book he's holding. "What's that?"

"This"—he holds it out to me—"is what we're going to do today, if you want to. I thought you might like it."

The cover has three very cool looking characters on it: a sexy girl elf, a dwarf with a long red beard in a business suit, and a vampire in a policeman's uniform. The title reads: *LARP of Ages.*

"I've heard of this. Live-action role playing, right? I think I've seen some videos on the internet. Guys dressed up, running around the woods, throwing ping-pong balls that are supposed to be lightning bolts at each other…"

"There's more to it than that," he says with a playful punch on my shoulder. "I thought we'd go down to the riverbank and create a character for you. Even if you don't want to go to a game and play with everyone else, creating a character is fun."

"I hate the riverbank."

He crooks an eyebrow at me. "Why?"

"I'm scared of the geese. When I was five, my mom took me down there to feed those horrible beasts and one of them nearly took my hand off." A shiver runs through my body just at the thought of those beady eyes focusing on the piece of bread I held in my hand. "I have a better place."

. . .

When we pull up to the aquarium, Logan says, "Nobody's here."

"Yeah, isn't it awesome? Terra and I always come here when we skip school."

We walk into the small reception area. They don't even have anybody who watches the place—it's just open to the general public. On the walls are posters of animals commonly found in Louisiana and a map of the fish hatchery that sits behind the aquarium. There is a guest book, though. I flip through the pages to a few weeks ago when Terra and I decided to take the day off from school. I point it out to Logan.

The corner of his mouth edges up. "Which one are you? BlairFanone or BlairFantwo?"

"Two. Terra's status as Allison's number one fan can never be challenged."

He laughs. "Of course, what was I thinking?"

The fish room is oval shaped and about as big as my living room, which isn't saying much. It's lined with aquariums that hold many creatures I could probably find in the pond by my grandparents' house. There's a lazy snapping turtle, a bass, and an enormous albino catfish that has been here forever. Terra and I dubbed him Mr. Whiskers at the beginning of the year.

Logan and I make the round going from glass to glass. The only light in the room comes from the aquariums. Distorted by the water, it reflects onto Logan's face, giving him his own energy signals.

Once we say hi to Mr. Whiskers, we take a seat on one of the two benches. Logan hands me a notebook. I open it to a blank page as he opens the LARP of Ages book.

"So, basically, there are a bunch of different types of creatures you can be. Depending on which creature you pick, you get a certain amount of points to spend on different attributes and items. I think you'd be a perfect elf. They're really fast and smart, so they tend to use a bow and arrows or magic, but they also have the potential to become voracious hand-to-hand fighters with knives or swords."

He speaks so fast my head is spinning. "Hold up, what are attributes?"

"You know, stuff like agility, appearance, strength."

"Oh," I say, feeling stupid.

He picks up right where he left off. He talks about the different powers I could have and the different items like armor or healing potions. After another hour and a half of me asking tons of questions, I have a character. She's an elven princess named Laowyn whose people have sent her out into the world to "discover" herself. And I love her and she's awesome. I even start to imagine her wardrobe.

Logan looks over my character sheet. "I think you're good to go. So"—he folds the sheet in half—"do you want to go to the game with me Saturday night?"

Silence settles in as I look around at our audience of aquatic creatures. My eyes linger on Mr. Whiskers, like maybe he'll notice me looking at him and tell me what I should do. His mouth opens and closes a few times like he's trying to answer me, but that doesn't help.

A week or two ago, this kind of thing would be so not doable. But, man, this sounds like fun. I mean, I've actually been inside The Phoenix three times now and my world hasn't imploded. It's just like NerdCon, I guess. There's no way I'll know anyone at this thing.

I turn to Logan, and he's folding and unfolding my character. I smack his hands.

"Don't do that, she's fragile." I take the paper from him. "How can she be ready for epic LARPing if she's all rumpled?"

"So, you'll go?" The hopefulness in his voice tips the scales.

"Yes, I'll go. But only if I get to dress up."

"You'll like it, I promise." He leans back against the wall with a satisfied sigh.

I watch Mr. Whiskers for a while. The water trickles in the aquariums. Everything is calm. Everything except my mind. It's charged with Awesome Logan electricity. I'm aware of every little detail of him: the weave of his jeans and the smudges of ink on his forefinger and thumb. Are those goose bumps on his arms? Are these goose bumps on mine?

This is such a strange feeling. I've never felt it before. My mind keeps telling me this is wrong, this could ruin everything, but I feel so right. To be here with him, to be me, to be me here with him, just to be.

"Let's play a game," he says, and I jump like I was just caught surfing the comic book database website.

"What game?" I ask.

"Top Two and This or That."

"What's that?"

"I'll start with a top two question, and you have to say what your top two of whatever is. Like 'What are your top two colors?' Mine are green and black, by the way, even though black technically isn't a color but an absence of color or light or something—" He catches himself babbling and shakes his head, but I could listen to him ramble for hours. "Anyway, after we both ask a top two question, then we switch to a this or that one that's like which thing do you prefer, this or that. All you have to do is answer honestly and as quickly as possible. If you ask out of turn, you must do a dare. Okay?"

"Sounds fun. Go for it."

He stands and puts his hands behind his back as he paces. "What are your top two movies?"

"*Scott Pilgrim vs. the World* and *Tangled*."

"*Tangled*? Really?" He raises an eyebrow.

I pull my legs up underneath me, crisscross applesauce. "Hey, don't mock me. You said to be honest."

He laughs and runs his fingers through his hair. "That I did. Your turn."

"Okay, top two desserts?"

"That's hard. I'll go with my mom's peanut butter cake and those little apple pies they have at gas stations."

"Really?" He could pick anything, and he goes with gas station pastries?

"I'm a simple guy with simple tastes." He shrugs.

I just shake my head and grin. He sits back down, and my knee touches his thigh. My grin disappears. He leans forward, puts his elbows on his knees, and tilts his head to look into my eyes. His face is so close I can see he wears contacts. So do I.

"Glasses or contacts, which do you prefer to wear?" he says, taking the words from my brain.

"Glasses. I still get the heebie-jeebies every morning when my finger gets close to my eyeball."

He laughs again. "Me, too."

"Marvel or DC?" I have a feeling which comic book publisher he'll choose.

"DC, definitely."

"I knew you were going to say that. You seem like a comic purist."

"Excuse me, some of the greatest fictional characters ever conceived have come out of DC. What does Marvel have? Wolverine? A hairy guy with claws? Come on."

"Okay then, Superman or Batman?" I say, trying to stump him.

"Nonapplicable, I'm a Green Lantern guy." His eyes widen, and he points a finger at me. "And you just asked out of turn."

"But you didn't answer with this or that."

"Doesn't matter, the question was invalid." He rubs his hands together. "Let's see."

I can feel my face warming up, but I can't stop smiling. What is he going to dare me to do? I know what Eric would dare me. It'd probably be something inappropriate. What would I do if Logan dared me to kiss him?

"I dare you to…"

He pauses, and I want him to say it. I want him to want a kiss, because I realize I'd do it so fast it'd make his head spin.

"I dare you to do your happy dance," he says instead.

"Happy dance?"

"Come on, everyone has a happy dance."

"But… I have to be extremely happy to do a happy dance. It's not something I can just, you know, jump into."

"How about I give you some inspiration." He pulls his phone out of his pocket and presses a few buttons. A song with an upbeat keyboard begins, and Logan stands up. The happy lyrics say something about a birdhouse and a bee. He waves his hand at me to follow. Bouncing on the balls of his feet, he looks at me expectantly.

I stand up to face him and try to sway a little. He shakes his head as he turns the volume up.

"I just can't, I'm not happy enough."

"Pretend like the Natchitoches Central Chiefs just won the Super Bowl." He bounces a little more enthusiastically.

"That's good, I guess." My sway becomes a little more pronounced. A smile takes hold, not because of the thought of the Chiefs winning the Super Bowl, but because Logan is such an awkward dancer. He's gone from bouncing to alternating snaps of his fingers as he bobs his head. Plus, he's a little off rhythm.

"There's a *Tangled* marathon on in two minutes!" He has to yell over the music now.

"That's better." I start nodding my head to the beat.

"It's Christmas! You just got your Hogwarts acceptance letter, a copy of *Action Comics* #1, and a brand new car that runs on water!"

"Hell yeah!" I scream and let go.

My arms wave over my head. I jump and spin. My ponytail whips around, sticking to my lips, but I don't care. I do the twist, and Logan does the robot. His ears are super red, and our breaths are turning into huffs. And yet, I can't stop. I just keep dancing and singing along until we both collapse on a bench, laughing uncontrollably.

When we're leaving, Logan pauses at the door, then doubles back.

"What is it?" I ask

He grabs the pen hanging by a chain above the guest book. "We forgot to sign."

"That one doesn't work, never has." I hand him a pen from my purse. He hunches over the book to write.

When I try to see what he wrote, he closes the book and waves toward the door. "Ladies first."

I laugh a little and shake my head as I go in front of him.

• • •

That evening, as I'm waiting for Logan's show to come on, Eric calls. It's weird because, when my song/ringtone plays, I automatically get all these happy feelings, and my stomach does somersaults. But, when I see who's calling me, my heart drops.

I need to handle this. I can't be hanging out with Logan, dancing with him and meeting his parents, and still technically be with Eric. It's not fair to either of them. But I'd be losing the cheerleader-dates-the-quarterback piece of my carefully crafted popular persona, and I'm not ready to risk it. Not yet.

I don't answer the phone.

#11

The next morning, I pull up to Terra's house and reach into the backseat to get the multitude of plastic bags containing things like glitter pens, poster board, white T-shirts, and rhinestones. Terra comes out before I get to her door, followed by Rayann.

I internally roll my eyes. It's not that I don't like Rayann... Okay, I don't like her. She's a drama pirate. I always picture her standing at the bow of a boat with one of those telescopes that stretch out. "Thar she blows! Looks like so-and-so has been seeing someone else behind her boyfriend's back, me matey." I've had this exact conversation with her at least three times this past school year, minus the pirate-isms.

"Did you get extra glue sticks?" Terra asks, her super-curly hair bouncing as she takes some bags from me.

"Yep."

"And glitter?"

"Yep," I say again as we go inside. I wave to Terra's mom as we cross through the living room.

"What about sparkles for the shirts?"

"Yep, I got everything on your list, and yes, I have my money for the ticket."

"Great, I'll put it in my account so I can be ready to clicky, clicky on the tour website and buy our tickets. Oh my God, this is going to be so amazing. Can you believe it? We are going to actually see Allison. In person. Hear her. With our own ears." Terra dumps the contents of the bags on the floor of her room.

I hold in the little comment I want to make about how we've always heard Allison with our own ears. "Yeah, it's going to be great." I'm trying to sound enthusiastic, but it just comes out kind of flat. "So when exactly is the concert? I keep forgetting."

She dives for the markers. "I've told you like a million times, Mad. It's not this Saturday or the next, the one after that. Only like two weeks away."

I nod slowly. Why does Saturday throw a switch in my head? It's no one's birthday, I don't think—

The room gets all swirly when it hits me. Oh crap. Double, triple, quadruple crap to the nth degree! The comic convention is in two weeks. And Logan only has a day pass for Saturday.

I'm the worst person ever. Which way do I go? On one side, I see my best friend all dressed up in her Allison Blair T-shirt and glitter on her eyelids. Rayann stands behind her looking like an extra from *The Pirates of the Caribbean*, taunting me with the knife she's about to plunge into Terra's back. On the other side is Logan, wearing his old black and white chucks and his Power Girl T-shirt, the V.I.P. Day Pass hanging around his neck. There's a showdown moment where Terra brandishes her Allison CDs like throwing stars and Logan whips out a Captain America shield.

That's when Rayann whispers something in Terra's ear. My best friend looks at me, eyes wide and shimmering with the tears that are about to fall. She knows. She knows I'm about to abandon her. For a guy, no less.

A disgusted shiver runs through me at the thought. I can't believe I'm even contemplating blowing her off to go with Logan. She's the sweetest person in the world, like a sister to me. It sucks, but I have to back out of NerdCon. I promised Terra I'd go with her, so I'm going. End of story.

"Did you hear Allison's dating that guy who dated Sandra Bullock?" Rayann asks as she opens the package of T-shirts.

Terra looks at her with big, glossy eyes. "No way, she's dating Ewan Cooper. They're perfect for each other."

"Well, that's what it said on SmashTalk.com," Rayann says smugly.

I pat Terra on the shoulder. "You know SmashTalk can never be believed. I mean, isn't that the same site that said Allison was really a terrorist using her music to brainwash teenagers with hidden messages?"

"Whatever." Rayann shrugs. "But they *were* seen canoodling last weekend."

Canoodling? Seriously? Terra just stares at the floor like it's about to drop out from under her.

"Don't worry about it," I tell her. "I'm sure it's just a rumor. Ewan Cooper will probably be at the concert. We'll have to keep an eye on the side of the stage." I open the glitter pens and hand her the pink one. "So, what's your shirt going to say?"

"I'm putting 'Number one Allison Fan,'" Rayann says.

When Terra's face falls even further, I want to smack Rayann. Terra flattens out a sheet of poster board, then pencils in some big bubble letters. Her brow furrows, and I'm pretty sure it's not because she's concentrating on drawing.

"Why don't we all put our favorite lyric on the front and 'I heart Allison' on the back?" I ask.

Terra perks up. "Oh, I like that! Or maybe, on the back, you could have 'I', Rayann could have a heart, and I could have 'Allison'. So when we stand next to each other it'll—"

Rayann cuts her off. "I want to be the 'Allison' part."

Terra narrows her eyes at her. "Fine. I'll be the heart."

"That'll work," I say, nodding like this is the best idea ever. "That way you can wear your shirt again."

Terra pulls out the masking tape, a little bit of her sparkle coming back. "How about we tape a bunch of poster boards together so we have this big, long sign we can all hold up?"

I ignore Rayann's scowl and keep going. "And we could make a cheer that involves the signs. Maybe Allison will hear it if we do it during a break in the music. We could ask someone to film us, too."

"Hello, YouTube gold! Perfect!" A happy grin on her face, Terra starts taping the boards together.

I should be happy I've managed to thwart the drama pirate and return my best friend to her happy place. And I am. But I can't stop a deep sigh from escaping as I reach for the bright blue rhinestones. Oh, NerdCon, your awesomeness will be missed.

Terra pops up. "I'm going to get my phone so we can listen

to Allison while we do this. Maybe the chant can have the same beat as one of her songs?"

I smile big and give her two thumbs up.

As soon as Terra leaves, Rayann turns on me. "What's going on with you? There's no way you're as excited about this concert as you're pretending to be. I've seen how bored you look when Terra starts talking about Allison. Just because she's not paying attention doesn't mean the rest of us aren't."

"Nothing's going on with me," I say maybe a little more cheerful than I normally would. The last thing I need is for her to think something is going on with me, and she just pulled out her telescope, I can feel it. "I'm just really excited about going to a live concert. And hanging out with you and Terra. Summer gets boring, you know?"

"If you say so," she says just before Terra returns and sits back down.

We all craft our hearts for a while until Terra asks, "So, where have you been, Maddie? Every time I text, you don't answer until it's too late to do anything."

"Yeah, Maddie," Rayann says. "If summer's been so *boring*, why haven't you been hanging out with us?"

I'm pretty sure I just became the big X on the treasure map. I have to come up with an excuse quick, and in the end, the one I come up with is pretty darn lame. "I've been helping my mom around the house, and the battery on my phone is really sucky so I have to leave it plugged in all the time. By the time she lets me hang out in my room, it's usually pretty late."

Terra looks thoughtful. "I could always just try your home phone. I don't know why I didn't think of that before."

"No!" What if she calls when I'm using her as an excuse to go be a geek with Logan? "I mean, Dad is always waiting on calls about new jobs. I can't even pick up the home phone without him telling me to put it back." I shrug and try to laugh again, but it just comes out as a wobbly flutter of sound.

Rayann smiles like I'm about to walk the plank, waiting for that moment I plummet to my death. Terra just looks kind of confused and goes back to her bubble letters.

Once my T-shirt looks only slightly better than the one I made in fourth grade during a Brownies meeting, I ask Terra, "Can I leave this here to dry? Mom would kill me if I got this glitter pen gel stuff all over the inside of my car."

"Sure."

"Thanks. Well, I have to head out. Mom probably has half a million things waiting for—"

Terra sits back on her heels, a frown on her face. "But what about the cheer? We haven't even started working on it yet."

I edge toward the door, wishing Rayann would stop with her smug looks. Could she just stop with her stupid face all together? "Later, I promise. I mean, how much help can my mom really need?"

"Okay," Terra says sadly, but when she stands, she turns back into giddy, hand-talking Terra. "This is going to be awesome. I can't wait! You're the best *ever*." She gives me a tight hug.

Oh yeah, I'm the *best,* all right. More like the girl who is so buried in lies she can't see through them enough to realize she almost broke her best friend's heart.

Rayann puts on a fake smile and holds her arms open for a hug, too. "Maybe your mom will let you hang out with us again soon," she whispers in my ear. Her tone isn't hopeful—it's freaking *sinister*. Like she can't wait for the next opportunity to catch me in a lie I can't talk my way out of.

I hurry out the door while I still can, chills skittering down my spine.

#12

"Mom, Terra and Rayann want to go to a late movie tonight. Can I go?" I call from my bedroom door.

Logan's show is almost over, and we're supposed to go to the LARP of Ages game tonight once he's finished. I told him I'd meet him at the radio station at around 9:30 so he could help me with my costume.

"What time is it over?" Mom yells back at me from downstairs.

"Supposed to be 11:30."

"Okay, just call when you're on your way home."

Geez, I hate lying to her, but the last thing I need is Mom chatting with her friends about my "new hobby." Plus, it's just a little white lie. No biggie. But if that's the case, why do I have to constantly tell myself to stop thinking about it?

I check myself in the mirror. I've decided to wear a cute full skirt that stops at my knees and a sheer blouse with a chemise underneath. My hair has been painstakingly curled to create a wavy mass. It's funny how it takes so much time and so many steps to make one's hair look effortless.

When I get to the radio station, I check the supplies I bought earlier along with the Allison Blair fan craft stuff. There are fake flowers, super glue, ribbon, ping-pong balls, blue face paint, crazy false eyelashes, and blue tights.

Sitting in my parked car, I fashion a choker out of the ribbon and glue some fake sunflowers onto it. I put another flower ribbon on my wrist. Another flower goes in my hair. I'm almost an elven princess.

As always, the second I start to feel happy about something and like everything might be okay after all, things I don't want to think about pop into my head. Things like I just straight up lied to Mom, which makes me a horrible daughter. And worse, I have to tell Logan I can't go to the convention.

And when I tell him why, there's a really good chance he'll say, "Screw you and the Lumina you rode in on." Or he might just put on some big, puppy-dog eyes and talk about all the things I'm going to miss. Good-bye, cosplay contest. Good-bye, having #400 signed by the author and the artist. Good-bye, getting my picture taken with Logan and Stan Lee. But I have to be up front with him.

So much for a fun, relaxing night of LARP.

The security light over the door to the college recording studio clicks on when Logan and another guy, I assume the mysterious Ben, step outside. I check my makeup in my rearview mirror. I'm going to have to redo it after the face paint, and yet, I still throw on some extra lip gloss.

I wait for Ben to get into his Jeep and drive off before I get out of the car. Logan stops midstep when he sees me. This shouldn't make me as happy as it does, especially not when I'm planning to give back my NerdCon pass as soon as he gets into my car.

"Wow, you are definitely elven royalty material," he says.

Maybe the NerdCon pass can wait a few more minutes.

"I can't believe I'm actually going to do this."

"You're going to love it, don't worry." We climb into my car, and he turns to me. "Thanks for the ride, by the way. Vera had swim lessons, Jonah wanted a ride to the library, Mom had grocery shopping to do, and Dad had the van at the shop, so it was just easier to let Mom take my car."

He's rambling again. I make a mental note to put a voice recording app on my phone so I can catch that brand of adorkableness next time.

"It's no problem at all."

On the drive to his house, the thought hits me I'm about to do one of the nerdiest things anyone can do. Dressing up as an elf princess so I can go frolic with other people pretending to be fantastical beasts? It's crazy, right?

But then it occurs to me I might not actually *get* to do this craziness because of the NerdCon thing. Might as well get that over with before I get too attached to my new life as an elf.

I take a deep breath and start rummaging in my purse while trying to also keep an eye on the road.

Then Logan starts going off about the game. "There was this one time when we had to go up against a gargoyle, which is one of the most powerful beings in the game, and I had to track him down because I was the only one who had this aura-identifying power," and on and on. He's so into it, it just makes me wish I could be that free. Free to talk about something other than Allison Blair without my friends looking at me like I screwed up the halftime dance routine. He finishes the story with lots of flailing and sound effects, and all I can do is grin, my fingertips grazing the VIP pass.

He sort of pushes my leg. "I'm just saying it's fun. You're going to love it." A goofy, endearing smile takes over his face as we pull into his driveway. He jumps out of the car and starts doing the robot with my low beams as his spotlight.

I can wait to tell him, I decide when he robot dances to my door to open it for me. He's too excited about this. Too sweet. If I can't go to the convention, I want to at least have this night with him. And I want it to be unmarred by my stupid lies and my all-around life suckiness.

I tuck the VIP pass deeper in my purse and force myself to forget it.

When we get inside, Martha is doing the dishes.

"Oh, Maddie, you look great. Give me a twirl." She swishes her finger in a circle, flinging soap bubbles onto the kitchen floor. I spin, and she applauds. "You must be from the Trulu race, right?"

"Yes, ma'am."

"Do you have blue paint?"

"Yes, ma'am."

"How about some black eyeliner for the ceremonial face tattoos?"

"Well, I have some in my purse I could—"

"Oh, honey, don't use your good stuff. I have some I put aside just for this kind of thing. It's in the drawer by the sink in the upstairs bathroom." She points at the ceiling.

Logan shows me to the upstairs bathroom and leaves to put on his own outfit. I put on the blue tights, stretching and yanking until they feel comfortable. The face paint isn't like a Smurf blue, thank goodness. It's more like a muted baby blue. It should be enough of a disguise so no one knows who I really am, especially since I'm adding these monstrous eyelashes and the ceremonial tattoos. It probably doesn't matter anyway. Logan said the majority of the players are college students.

I'm just finishing up drawing my tattoos, pretty swirls that seem to flow from my eyes, when Logan appears in the doorway over my shoulder in the mirror. I stop midswirly.

He's wearing black jeans and an amazingly hot black biker jacket over a white T-shirt. His normally casual bedhead hair is now perfectly styled bedhead hair. He also has light blue skin, but his tattoos are understated, just dots in a straight line that go from ear to ear crossing the bridge of his nose. He props himself against the door frame, and my mind goes blank.

"I like the viney things you have going on there."

I clear my throat because it has suddenly gone dry. "Thanks. You look very…" I trail off because I almost said elf-a-licious. "Very believable."

"I *have* done this more than a few times." He grins. I feel a twinge of anger at myself for missing all those more than a few times.

"You never told me you were a Trulu, too."

He steps into the bathroom, which is pretty small, so he's

only about a foot and a half behind me. There goes my heart again, thrumming inside my chest so hard I can feel it in my ears.

"I just made the character today. I figured it would make more sense if we were of the same race because I'll probably be around you a lot."

"My hero," I say in a breathy voice.

"Not that you wouldn't be able to handle yourself, but…" He rolls his eyes. "You ready?"

• • •

We decide to ride together in his car because he's trying to be a gentleman. We turn down a street lined with big, beautiful houses all with enormous doors and topiaries that guard the driveways.

"I told Dan he could ride with us. I hope that's okay?"

"Of course." The guy has already heard me belch. I don't think him seeing me in elf garb could be any more embarrassing than that, even if he thought it was Logan belching and not me.

As we pull up to one of the biggest houses I've ever seen this close, I try to list all the people who know about my double life in my head. I can only think of three: Logan, Dan, and Martha who, let's face it, doesn't seem like the type to go around gossiping about the activities of the girl who's hanging out with her son. This is good. This is manageable. If I can keep it down to only these few people, who knows how long I can continue to indulge in being nerdy-me and all the perks that come with it.

Dan barrels out of his front door carrying two twelve packs of sodas and what looks like a tree limb tucked under his arm. He's kind of chunky, but he has a nice face. I bet he's going to be one of those guys that just gets better looking as time goes by. It's his vocabulary that needs work.

"Can I get some help with this shit?" he yells.

I get out of the car and take one of the cases of sodas. Logan pops the trunk so we can stash them back there. That's when I realize what the tree limb actually is. Dan props the tip of his gigantor foam sword wrapped in duct tape on the ground. His hand is wrapped around the hilt which is next to his cheek. Dan is only an inch or two shorter than me, so, yeah, that's a really, really long sword.

When I pull my eyes away from it, I realize he's looking me up and down.

"Damn, girl," he says, and I don't hide my eye roll. "I would get in trouble for saying this if my clan ever found out, but you look freaking fine tonight."

I cross my arms. "Wait, your clan? What are you?"

"What?" he yells in the deepest voice he can manage. "I take offense to your ignorance, elfling." He tries to brandish his sword, but it knocks against the car.

"Who are you calling 'elfling'? I'm over two hundred years old."

"Bah, that's a drop in the bucket for a dwarf. You will regret—"

"Hey," Logan says as he leans over the top of his car. "No gaming outside of the venue without a sanctioned game master. Leave her alone, Dan."

"Chill out, dude. I was just having some fun," he says, then turns to me. "Way to stick up for yourself. When you're a new player at these things, you must prepare to be tested."

"Thanks," I say, feeling extremely proud of myself.

"I have just one more thing to say to you, elf."

"Oh yeah, what's that, dwarf?"

"Shotgun!" Dan cackles as he clomps around to the front passenger door like a kid wearing his father's boots. They look like they weigh a ton each and have spikes sticking up from the toes that are obviously just foam as well. He also has shoulder pads that have the same foam spikes pointing in all directions.

"No, dude, I veto your shotgun," Logan says.

"Aw, come on, why?"

"Because, I'm not having that ridiculous sword knocking my rearview mirror around."

I open the back door for Dan and give him a grand bow.

Dan gives me an evil stare. "I see what's going on here. The Trulus sticking together. It's racist, that's what it is!"

#13

"I can't believe everyone has to play with a new character this year. I've been playing Craytor for like two years. He's such a badass now," Dan says as he leans forward and props his elbows on our seats.

"I think it's a great idea," Logan says. "We need some new blood, and people never stick around long if their new characters can't hang with the more experienced ones. Besides, you'll be able to bring Craytor back three times over the summer, I think."

"Why is Craytor such a badass?" I ask.

"Your character gets points for every game session they participate in," Dan says. "Plus, there's a chance for bonus points if you do some extra special stuff during a game. You can then use those points to increase attributes or powers or buy items. And Craytor was the man last year. Remember when I took down that chimera all by myself, dude, while all you guys decided to run and—"

"Yes, I remember. I was there. And you've told me the story about a million times since then," Logan says.

"Well, it's like my dear old grandma always says, 'If you never get told you're a wuss, you'll always be a wuss,'" Dan says.

"I know your grandma, and she would never say that," Logan says.

"Hey, my MeeMaw is a tough old bird. Don't underestimate her."

I swear, these two fight like a married couple. When we get to the gaming venue—which turns out to be just the backyard of the game master's house—the butterflies that have been building in my stomach turn into a swarm of angry pixies.

Logan and Dan get out of the car to get the sodas from the trunk, but I stay put. There are so many people here we had to park on the side of the road. All types of otherworldly creatures meander around the house.

How could I ever have considered this? I have no idea how to play this game. What if my character gets killed? In the first game, no less? I'll be the dumbest nerd who ever nerded.

"You ready?" Logan says when he opens my door.

"I don't know if this is such a good idea," I say.

"You'll be fine." He holds out a blue tinted hand. He looks at me with eyes that seem to be bluer than ever because of his face paint. His smile isn't the knowing one I've come to expect. It's gentle and confident.

I take his hand and don't let go as we walk into the mass of role players.

We go through the front door which has a sign taped to it

that reads:

> You are about to enter a nightclub for
> paranormal creatures called Sanctuary, which
> means stepping over this threshold puts you IN
> ## GAME:
>
> **Rule #1:** No drinking or drugs allowed. Anyone
> suspected of being under the influence will be
> ejected from the game.
>
> **Rule #2:** Leave your true self at the door. Do not
> drag out-of-game events and feelings into the game.
> Just because so-and-so stole your girlfriend does
> not mean your character will also want to rip so-
> and-so to shreds.
>
> **Rule #3:** If you need to run a scene that involves
> attributes, powers, or items, please find a game
> master to oversee. Let's keep things official.
>
> **Rule #4:** Be respectful to others and HAVE FUN!

As we make our way through the front room toward the
kitchen, my eyes don't know where to look. Dwarves, vampires,
shape-shifters, bright fairies, dark fairies, werewolves, and
creatures I can't even put a name to mill about all over the place.
In the kitchen, Logan and Dan add their sodas to a growing pile
of other drinks and snacks. We head toward the back door but
have to wait for some type of dragon guy with a long, lumpy tail
to go by before we can go through to the gaming venue.

Moody, almost hypnotizing music washes over me as I step
into the thick grass. A towering magnolia tree grows in the

middle of the yard. From it hangs an enormous, rotating disco ball that reflects dots of light onto many more gamers. It looks like creatures of the same race are splitting up into groups. In a back corner of the yard, there's a group of glittery fairies wearing sparkly mesh wings. They look so pretty, I make a mental note to search for fairy costumes this coming Halloween.

In the completely opposite corner, closer to the house, is a group of dark fairies. They're all dressed in black with black hair, black eye shadow, black lips, and torn black wings. Just black all over. I make eye contact with one of these fairies, and she scowls. Her charcoal-encircled eyes narrow, and her deathly lips form a snarl. I immediately look away because I'm actually frightened. I can almost feel the animosity rolling off this chick.

When I look at Logan, he smiles down at me and squeezes my hand, which he has thankfully yet to let go of.

"Brothers, ho!" Dan yells and stomps across the yard to a group dwarves also covered in foam spikes. He's met with elaborate handshakes and chest pounds and head slams.

"Come on, dude, I have neighbors," a guy standing next to us in a flowing, dark green robe and sporting an extremely fake, white beard, says to Dan.

Logan leads me to a couple of lawn chairs on the edge of the yard. When we sit, he says, "See, not so crazy, is it?"

I let out a nervous laugh. "Of course not. This is all completely normal."

"Just relax. Remember, you're an elven princess. Get into your character."

"Right, right." My name is Laowyn. I am the heir to a throne. I should sit straight and cross my ankles. I'm prissy, but not snobby. I'm naive about the world outside my kingdom.

"By the way, I added something to your character sheet in the history section, so it would be more believable that you're here tonight."

He hands me my character sheet, and I scan it over to find the history. Tacked onto the last paragraph I wrote is a sentence in Logan's handwriting which is small and precise, easy to read. It says: *Laowyn is in a relationship with Graffin.*

"Oh really, Graffin?" I look at him out of the corner of my eye.

"You had to have a reason to be here tonight. Your character wouldn't have had any clue this was a club for our kind. I figure our parents could have known each other and introduced us." When I don't immediately say anything, he fiddles with the zipper of his jacket and says, "Don't worry, it's only a game. We just have to pretend to be together."

It's a good thing I'm wearing blue paint because I can feel my cheeks heat up. I glance at his hands. He can't stop fiddling with the zipper. When I try to make eye contact, he avoids looking at me. His zipper must be really awesome.

I nudge his arm with my elbow. "Okay. Gotta keep things believable, right?"

"Right. It's all to make things as real as possible."

His shoulders relax, and he lays his arm across the back of my chair. He fidgets a little more, his fingers drumming a rhythm on the back of my chair, then drops his arm back down to his side. It's adorable, really. I scoot my chair closer to him and wrap my arm around his elbow, smiling up at him as coyly as I can while batting my super-long eyelashes. He laughs that honest laugh.

"Have you ever done this before? Had your character in a relationship?" I ask. "It seems like such a professional gamer thing to do."

"I, uh — " His gaze darts to the group of dark fairies. He opens his mouth to continue, but the music stops. Everyone around us begins to move to surround the tree, but I can see someone trying to fight through the stream of people. That scary dark fairy has her evil eyes trained on Logan and me as she weaves through the crowd.

"Looks like things are about to get going. Let's go see what Tommy, I mean, game master Sorenson has to say," Logan says. He stands, and I follow him into the crush of people.

By the time everyone settles down, the evil fairy is nowhere in our vicinity. I relax slightly.

The Dumbledore wannabe from earlier climbs onto a coffee table that's been placed in front of the tree. He holds his hands up for quiet, and I have to admit it's pretty cool when everyone goes silent.

"Welcome to every one of you, new and old," he says in a decent English accent. "I hope you've all come to Sanctuary tonight to have some civilized fun, because we have an interesting evening in store for you." He ends with a flourish of his robe, and the crowd erupts into applause.

He drops the accent and says, "If you have Area Knowledge under your specialties, see game master Torrak." He motions to one of Dan's clansman. "That's it, and remember the rules, folks."

People spread out. Some dance to the music that has taken an upswing in tempo, but most form the same groups as before. Logan takes me with him to Torrak because he has the area knowledge thing. He says his character would tell my character everything he knows anyway so I might as well hear it straight from the dwarf's mouth.

Torrak has spared no expense on his getup. His foot-long red beard looks freakishly real. The plate of armor covering his chest could have been picked up at the Lord of the Rings garage sale.

A sickly-looking vampire who smells like baby powder gets to Torrak first, so we hang back and wait our turn. I take the moment to do some more creature-watching, which turns out to be a bad idea. Everyone here seems so comfortable in their fake skins. It's intimidating and wonderful, and I want to be just like them. But I keep thinking I don't deserve to be here. If these people knew how ashamed I've been that I'm like them, they wouldn't accept me. They'd dub me an imposter, a poseur. My gaze drifts to Logan's face. It's overly scrunched up in a worried look which makes me realize he's mimicking my own expression. I force my brows to unknit and try to put on a relaxed smile.

He steps closer to me and takes my hand. Instead of a normal, friendly handhold, he laces his fingers between mine. I don't know if it's real or just my imagination, but the warmth that travels from our interlocked fingers, up my arm, and over my whole body makes all the tension in my muscles melt away.

Finally, the vampire leaves, and we step up. Torrak pounds his chest with a closed fist and says, "Ho, friends." He tells us there have been some abnormal events going on in the city. Random human citizens have been committing crimes that just don't fit with who they are. Stay-at-home moms are robbing banks. Upstanding business men have been caught shoplifting makeup. The drunk tank at the police station has become so full of old ladies they had to empty the public swimming pool to make room for more wasted grandmothers. The insanity is escalating. Rumors are circulating amongst the paranormal community that one of our own is responsible.

As we walk away to let a guy with a sign on his back that reads "I'm a Centaur" hear the information, I ask Logan, "Okay, so what do we do now?"

"We mingle, we chitchat, we try to find out what other people know. Looks like it's going to be a good old-fashioned whodunnit this summer."

"Well, if we already know that's it's one of us doing this stuff…" I look up at Logan. One of his eyebrows raises, and the corner of his mouth quirks up. "Um, wouldn't we try to find out who can control humans like that? Make humans do things they wouldn't want to do."

"Wait, let me see your character sheet." I hand it to him. "I thought so. You have a nice level of Race Knowledge. I guess you spent a lot of those two hundred years in the library while you were stuck in your parents' castle. Let's go talk to Torrak and see if we can find out some more."

We pull Torrak aside, and Logan nudges me. "Go on, ask him."

"Okay, um, I have this Race Knowledge thing and—"

"Well done." Torrak leans in close to whisper, "You would know certain races have the ability to control humans' actions. You would also know dark fairies are one of these races, and they have a tendency to enjoy chaos and pranks."

My eyes go wide. "Okay, thanks."

Torrak nods and goes back to his clan.

Logan throws his arm around my shoulders and squeezes. "Good job. I bet we know more than anyone else. Knowledge is power, right? Let's get a soda."

We move over to the refreshment table. There are chips and dip, cookies, and candy. There's also an array of sodas, all caffeinated. These people are going to be wired by night's end if this is all there is to snack on.

"Hi, Logan," a silky voice says from behind us. Logan's hand, which is in the middle of pouring his soda into a cup of ice, jerks, sloshing brown liquid onto my open-toed shoes.

"Oh crap. Sorry, Mad, I mean, Laowyn." He rips off a paper towel from the roll on the foldout table and tries to clean off my shoes.

"Logan?" the voice says again, and I turn. It's her, the dark fairy that's been giving me the willies all night. The second we make eye contact, the corner of her top lip twitches like she's fighting the urge to growl.

"Hey, Kelsey, how's it going?" Logan says.

"Can I talk to you for a minute?" She puts a hand on his forearm. "Alone?"

Now I feel my own growl creep up in my throat.

Logan steps away from her. "We're in the middle of game here. Can't it wait?"

"No," she says, her tone impatient. "It'll just take a second, I promise. It's important."

He lets out a long sigh and turns to me. "I'll be right back, okay?"

"Sure," I say in my it's-not-okay-but-I'm-going-to-say-it-is-anyway voice.

Her jet black bob swishes and her wings smack me in the face when she turns to go to the other side of the house with Logan in tow. I pretend my eyes are girlifying lasers and concentrate on her. Unfortunately, she doesn't turn into a Barbie look-alike, but I imagine what her reaction would be anyway: Terror, horror, and ultimately, running away screaming.

"What'd she want?" Dan says as he walks up.

"To talk. Alone."

"Poor Logan. He has the worst luck with girls," he says. "I guess we all can't be as discerning as myself."

"What do you mean?"

"I mean I am single by choice, not because no girl will have me." He points a finger at me like he's making a very valid statement.

I give him a long blank stare, but he doesn't get the hint. "I meant, what do you mean about Logan having the worst luck with girls?"

"Well, that girl"—he nods in the direction Logan and Kelsey just went—"kind of drug him through the mud, then broke his heart. She bossed him around all the freaking time, put him down, told him he needed to get out of the comic shop and start a band or something like that. She just wanted him to do it because her roommate at that smart kid school had a boyfriend who was in a band. But Logan doesn't have a clue about how to make music, just how to announce it. The crazy thing is he didn't really mind being bossed around and stuff. The straw that broke the camel's back was the lying. See, she did end up with a guy in a band. Her roommate's guy, actually. And she accomplished all that while she was still with Logan."

"What a bitch." The words pop out of my mouth before I can stop them.

"You said it. But then again, at least she wasn't ashamed of him."

I watch his back as he walks away. What was *that* supposed to mean? Then my brain catches up. Aren't I in the process of dragging him through the mud in exactly the same way?

Logan appears from around the corner of the house, his head dipped as he rubs the back of his neck.

"You ready to go?" he says when he reaches me.

"But we've only been here for, like, thirty minutes."

"We've done all we can do. The first game is always slow anyway."

I wouldn't know since this *is* my first game. "Are you okay?" I try to touch his forearm, but he dodges me. Over Logan's shoulder, I catch Kelsey watching us with a smirk.

"I'm fine. It's just…" He looks at me like he's waiting for me to say something specific, something profound. I guess my expression of utter confusion isn't what he's hoping for. "I'm just tired. All day at the shop, then the show for two hours."

"What about Dan?"

"I'll go tell him. He'll probably just find a ride."

Ten minutes later, we're heading back up the street and toward his house. It's quiet for a long time before I can't stand it anymore.

"Are you sure you're okay?"

"Fine."

He doesn't say another word, and I'm not going to force him to talk if he doesn't want to. It's probably best to just leave him alone. It's not like I should even be *allowed* to help him feel better. If what Dan says is true, I should just walk away before I turn into Kelsey. She straight up used him. I'm using him—sort of, though not for nefarious means or anything—*and* lying to everyone around me about who he is, who I am, and where we go when I'm with him. We pull up next to my car, and there's a long, uncomfortable silence before I say, "Well, I guess I'll talk to you later."

I go to open the door, but Logan says, "What's going on here?"

"What do you mean?" I scrunch up my face. The face paint has hardened so it's just as uncomfortable as the question he just asked.

"There are some wet wipes in the glove compartment. What I mean is what are we doing? Is this like just some summer experiment to you or…" He trails off and looks out his window.

The accusation is like a punch to the gut. Because he's totally right. I have been treating this like Las Vegas: what happens in the summer, stays in the summer.

I start scrubbing at my face and hands with the wipes, mostly so I don't have to look him in the eye. "Was it that girl? Did she say something about me?" I can hear the defensiveness in my voice.

"Don't worry about her," he says. "What I mean to say is could you ever see me as… There have been some moments between us, right? I know I'm not imagining them."

In a span of seconds, those "moments" flash through my mind. Not only do I remember that day in The Phoenix when I was dying to read #400 and our impromptu happy dance in front of Mr. Whiskers, but I also remember moments he doesn't know about. Like the time I watched him try and fail to open his locker for five minutes, then spent the rest of that day fantasizing about what would have happened if I had gone over and helped him. Or when I talked the squad into cheering at a soccer game just so I'd have a reason to see him play.

But those memories are quickly replaced with moments that haven't happened yet. Moments like seeing Logan in the hall on the first day of senior year and having to pretend I don't know him. Rayann asking, "Who was that?" and me answering, "I have no idea."

I don't want to do that to him. Which is why I say, "No. No moments. I have a boyfriend. You know this, Logan."

His lips slowly tighten into a thin line. "Just... Whatever. It doesn't matter." He sounds so angry, so hurt. He climbs out of the car and slams the door. If that isn't a screw-you, I don't know what is. He doesn't even turn around to make sure I get out of his car. Just strides up the steps to his house and disappears inside.

By the time I finally get into my car and dig through my purse looking for something to help with this paint, my hands are shaking. Logan's the first person outside of my family to accept me for who I am, and I've stomped all over him. The NerdCon pass surfaces with the package of tissue I find, and I look at the ceiling of my car, wishing I wasn't such a jerk. Logan's pissed at me, and rightfully so, but it looks like I'm not done dragging him through the mud yet.

As I walk back to Logan's car, my feet feel so heavy I actually look down to make sure I'm not wearing Dan's boots. This is tough because giving the pass back this way means we probably won't have any more contact other than the occasional awkward run-in at school. For a second, I look back at his house, wishing he'd come back, but that would just make this harder.

I open the car door, drop the pass on the seat, and leave.

#14

Mom is sleeping on the couch in her grandma nightgown when I get home. I sneak upstairs to wash all the stupid Smurf paint off and change into pajamas. Mom always complains the next day about muscle cramps if she sleeps all night on the couch, so I tiptoe back downstairs to wake her up.

"Mom," I whisper and shake her shoulder. "I'm home. Go to bed."

She snorts lightly, and her eyes pop open. She always wakes up like this, which freaks me out at first, and then I have to giggle, but tonight, at this moment, nothing is funny.

"Hey, honey, did you have a good time?" she says sluggishly.

"Yeah, I guess."

"What happened?" she says in that mom-way, like she knows something is wrong.

"Nothing." I put on an oblivious face. "Nothing happened.

Go to bed, okay?"

"Are you sure?"

I start to tell her I'm sure, that nothing happened, but she knows me better than anyone.

"Something happened. You want to talk about it?"

Yes! I would love to talk about it. I can feel the words bubbling up. It's crazy how Mom has a way of pulling things out of me, but I can't admit I lied to her about where I was going tonight. So, I try to tell her only the parts she needs to know.

"There's this guy," I say.

"Ah, I think I know where this is going." She sits up and settles in to listen.

"I mean, I know I'm with Eric right now, and he's awesome. Well, kind of. In a superficial sort of way." I frown. Wow. *How do you really feel, Maddie?* "Anyway, I feel bad because I really like this other guy. He's funny, and we have a lot in common and—"

"Like what?"

Think fast. Do not confess how much or Mom will be all over you. "Uh, like, we're both going to be in honors classes next year."

"A smart guy. I like it."

"Yeah, but Eric is in Florida, and he won't be back for at least another two or three weeks. I don't want to break up with him over the phone, you know." And there it is. Mom has once again tugged out a truth I myself didn't even know existed. I let out a deep sigh I've been holding in ever since Logan suggested he was just my summer experiment.

"Do you want my advice?" Mom always says this because we used to fight all the time over her giving me her opinion about clothes, nail polish, or whatever when I really didn't want it.

"Yes, Mom, I want your advice." After the last big fight we had, we made an agreement: she would have to ask the question and I would have to actually say these words in order for her to continue.

"I know you don't want to break up with Eric over the phone, but if you intend on spending time with this new guy, then you need to call Eric. Either that or tell this new guy he can wait until Eric gets back and you can break up with him properly. It's all about how you treat people. You have to be considerate of Eric's feelings."

Of course, this is exactly what I didn't want to hear, but Mom's right. This has to be done.

• • •

In the morning, I pick up my phone to call Eric, but I just stare at the screen. Am I really about to do this? Break up with the most wanted guy in school for Logan, a guy I've only really known for not even two weeks? Mom's right, but what will this really accomplish? I'll ruin Eric's vacation. How can that be the best thing to do?

The only other option sucks. Ask Logan to "wait for me" until Eric gets back? What is this? The fifties?

I put my phone down and try to do normal, everyday things. Maybe if I give the problem a little breathing room, it'll work itself out.

Yeah, right.

I'm doing the dishes when I catch myself staring out the window, wondering what Logan is doing at that very second.

As I fold clothes with Mom, we watch her soap opera which incites images of Eric freaking out after my call. Would he be so distraught he would throw himself off a pier, all the while professing his love for me? I doubt it. We're not in love. He knows it. I know it.

I go through this same cycle for the entire day, plus most of the next. It's around 6:30 that next evening when I finally decide to really analyze the situation.

Approaching this as scientifically as possible, I open a blank document on my laptop and set up two pros and cons lists, one each for Logan and Eric. When I'm done, the scales are obviously tipped. The best pro I can come up with for Eric is he washed my car for me two months ago. That is nothing compared to Logan being a horrid dancer, which I consider a pro because it's adorable.

My decision is made.

I call Eric immediately before my courage fades, but surprise, surprise, he doesn't answer.

"Hey, Eric," I say to his voice mail. "I wanted to let you know that I, um… The thing is… We need to talk. About important stuff. Relationship stuff. Like, whether or not we should be together stuff, because I don't think we should be. So yeah. Um. Give me a call as soon as possible, please?"

When I hang up, all I can think is, *Oh yeah, Maddie, 'please' is really going to lessen the blow. Great job!* But a big weight does feel like it's been lifted. It's done. Eric and I are finished. Now to talk to Logan and beg for forgiveness.

· · ·

The radio station is tucked in the middle of the campus in a small brick building surrounded by the Keyser Hall and Rapides dorms. Logan's is the only other car in the lot. I'm sitting in the same spot where I parked only two nights ago.

He's in there right now, probably shuffling through CDs, pressing buttons, or whatever it is he's supposed to do to get ready for his show. Maybe I should wait and talk to him later. Is being a disc jockey like being a football player? Do they have to get all testoteroned out and focused before air-time? Would I throw him off his voice-game? Could I wait until tomorrow? No, definitely not.

A Jeep whips into the parking lot, and out hops Ben. He's a short, black guy with down-to-his-waist long dreadlocks. He fast-walks toward the door, but I call to him before he gets there.

"Ben?"

"Yeah?" He skids to a halt.

"Hi, I'm here to talk to Logan real quick. Can you show me where—"

His brows furrow. "You're the cheerleader, right?"

"I'm *a* cheerleader. I don't know if I'm *the* cheerleader."

He crosses his arms and leans back a little as he looks at me like he's sizing me up. I suddenly wish I'd put a little more effort into my outfit. A T-shirt, jeans, and flip-flops doesn't exactly scream, "I'm the woman of his dreams."

"All right," he says after a few seconds. "I probably shouldn't allow this, but I need my talent to be happy. You *are* here to make him happy, right?" He points a scolding finger at me.

I straighten my back. "Yes."

He nods once and continues on to the door. I follow him

down a skinny hallway. The walls are cinder blocks painted in a glossy white and the carpet is the same low-quality kind that's in every school. The place smells like dust and Cup O Noodles.

Ben leads me to a small room that looks like every radio station I've ever seen in the movies, except not as glamorous. It's cramped and very dark. The control board or whatever you call it looks like it needs some work. Some of the knobs are missing. The Plexiglas window that separates us from the deejay booth is dull and could use a good long soak in a Windex bubble bath. I can see Logan through it, though. He's sitting at a crescent-shaped table with headphones on, flipping through a stack of CDs. My heart squeezes, then goes into overdrive at the sight of him.

Ben knocks on the window, bringing me back to my senses. Logan looks up from his CDs at Ben, then squints at me, trying to see through the horrible window, I guess. He picks up his glasses from the table and shoves them on his face. My stomach flutters, and my knees go a little weak. Who knew glasses could be so sexy? I try to smile and wave, but I'm sure I just look like I'm in pain. Behind the black-rimmed glasses, his eyes grow large.

We stay like that for what feels like eternity, Logan just staring and me with my hand suspended in the air, a questioning grimace on my face. Finally, he blinks a few times and waves for me to come in. I can feel a real honest-to-God smile take over my lips.

Ben leans over a microphone and presses a button. "You have less than two minutes until we go live."

Logan nods but continues to wave me in. I stumble over the leg of a rolling chair that's pushed up to the control panel as I head for the little swinging door that leads into Logan's booth. I thank all that is good and holy when I don't face plant into the wall.

When I finally make it inside, Logan stands. "What are you doing here, Maddie?"

My heart squeezes again at the sound of my name. "I wanted to talk to you. About the other night."

He doesn't respond, just keeps flipping through the CDs.

"Dude, one minute," Ben's voice says from somewhere above me. I look up to see an old box speaker hanging on the wall.

"I'm coming, I'm coming." Logan picks up a tall stack of CDs, using his chin to help balance them against his chest, and stomps toward me. I plaster myself to the wall on my right so he can shove the CDs through the door and into Ben's waiting hands.

"Here's the playing order." Logan pulls a sheet of paper out of his back pocket and hands it to Ben. He closes the door and turns to me. How close we are now reminds me of the aquarium, of how I could see his contacts. But, this time, his lips are tight.

"What is it?"

The dusty smell disappears to be replaced by his smell. If it's a cologne, it's a subtle one. Maybe it's his soap. Whatever it is, it smells really, really good. Kind of earthy but clean. I suddenly have the urge to bury my face against his neck and take a deep whiff.

"Come on, dude. Let's get a move on," Ben's voice says from above us again.

Logan raises his eyebrows in a silent, "Well?"

"I like your glasses." That's it. That's all I can say. It's all his fault, really. Obviously, my brain is not able to function properly when he's this close.

His stance relaxes as he lets out a long, slow breath. "You want to sit?" He reaches over and pulls a rolling stool up next to him, sits in his seat, then puts on his headphones.

When I sit down, our knees bang together. I try to say I'm sorry, but he just *shhh*-es me. I'm about to scoot away and give him his space when he shoves another set of headphones at me. I slip them over my ears, thinking how nice he is for wanting me to be able to hear the music.

Ben's voice echos through the headphones, "Five… Four… Three…" Through the window, I watch him hold up two fingers, then one, and then he points at Logan.

The ceiling light above us flickers, then dims as Logan leans toward the microphone on the table. Looks like this place could use some electrical wiring work, too.

"Hello, everyone, and welcome to another broadcast of Logan's Show of Awesome. We have some spectacular music planned for tonight, as always, but tonight is special, folks."

I lean forward and prop my chin on my fist, letting his voice melt over me.

"Tonight, I have someone I'd like you to meet."

The words take a while to register in my mind. I sit up and stare at him. Slowly, that knowing smile I've grown accustomed to creeps across his lips.

"Say hi to the awesome listeners, Wonderful Wendy."

#15

Logan pushes the microphone on its stand toward me. I look from him to the mic, then shake my head. He nods. I shake my head more fiercely, but he nods more. I mouth the words "I hate you," and he grins.

"Hi," I say into the mic, but I'm apparently too close. Logan jumps and scoots the mic away a little. "Sorry," I whisper.

He leans in to speak. "So, Wonderful Wendy, what has been awesome about your day?"

I get close to the microphone, too, expecting him to move back, but he doesn't. "Nothing really."

"Come on, something had to be awesome."

I shake my head.

He points at the mic.

"Nope, nothing."

"That's too bad, but then again, life is all about yin and yang, right? Things can't always be awesome. So, let's go with that. What was so not awesome about your day?"

I make sure to keep my eyes on his as I speak. "Well, I've been feeling bad about hurting someone. I said something I really didn't mean, and now this person probably hates me, which sucks. A lot. This person was right, and I should have admitted it."

A few seconds of silence goes by. We're sitting so close our knees are not only touching but are interlaced.

"That does suck." The way he says it is like he's not speaking to the audience. He's talking just to me. "What do y'all think, listeners? Got any advice for Wonderful Wendy or want to commiserate? Give us a call."

Logan flips a switch on the microphone, and a haunting woman's voice begins to sing through my headphones. He moves one side of his headphones off his ear, and I do the same.

"So?" He doesn't sound accusatory anymore. He sounds more...hopeful.

"You were right. There have been moments between us." I look down at our knees and notice a worn hole in his jeans. I touch the exposed skin with the tip of my finger.

"And?"

I tap my foot, anxious about what he'll think of this next part. "And... If you're willing to forgive me, I'd like for there to be more of our moments."

"So, you and Eric? Is there still a you and Eric?"

"Nope, that's over." Eric has to have listened to the voice mail by now and is too busy having fun to call back. I didn't expect him to be very concerned about us breaking up. There are plenty of other cheerleaders to act as his arm candy, thank God.

A crease forms between Logan's brows. Maybe it's the heartbreaking ambiance the music is creating, but I get this feeling like he wants to reveal something important.

"Maddie, I have to tell you…" He leans even closer to me and whispers, "I've…"

"Yeah?"

"I've… Never been lucky. With girls. With relationships. That whole thing. I guess, maybe, I overreacted the other night. I'm sorry. It's just, you're you, you know?"

"You didn't overreact. I was being a jerk."

He frowns even harder and opens his mouth like he's about comfort me, tell me I wasn't being a horrible person, but I shake my head.

It takes me a bit to get my words straight. "I like you, Logan. I like who I am when I'm around you. You're fun and considerate. And I trampled all over that. Like you said. I'm me and I'm trying to…fix that, but — "

He holds up his hand for me to stop. "No, that's not what I meant. I didn't mean it in a bad way. At all." He emphasizes those last two words and covers my hand with his, his thumb rubbing slightly, soothingly. "Let's just…forget all that even happened. Okay?"

Ben's voice buzzes over the speaker, and we both jump, "And we're back in five, four, three…"

Logan doesn't miss a beat. "Man, I love that song. What about you, Wonderful Wendy?"

I grin. "One of my favorites."

Ben waves at us and makes the international hand gesture

for *phone* with his thumb and pinky finger.

"Looks like we have a caller. Hello, awesome listener, what's your name?" Logan says.

"Hey, Awesome Logan. This is Dan-the-man."

Logan rolls his eyes but keeps his voice steady. "All right, Dan-the-man, what's on your mind?"

"Well, Awesome Logan, there are always a lot of things on my mind, because I'm extremely intelligent and always contemplative, a sort of modern-day philosopher, if you will, but at the moment, the main thing I'm thinking about is what I'd like to say to this chick you have cohosting with you even though you've never had a cohost and have probably had a close friend or acquaintance suggest that they cohost, but of course, you turned them down, which is a big, fat load of—"

"Thanks for calling in, Dan-the-man. We're going to take a quick break before you make your statement to Wonderful Wendy since I'm sure you'd like a little more time to think of the right way to put it. Have a quick listen to this piece about the upcoming NU production of *West Side Story*, audience." Logan cues Ben to play the segment.

"Dan, I told you not to call in because this is what always happens," Logan says, and I realize we can still talk to a caller while the music plays without it being broadcast. "This is a PG-rated show, and you have difficulty saying two words without one of them having something to do with inappropriate parts of an animal's body."

"How could I not call in? I asked you just the other day if I could be your cohost, and you said you couldn't have one, that it was against the rules. I am not happy with you, Awesome Logan, not happy at all. And don't think for a second I'm fooled by that codename bull-pucky. I know that's the cheerleader."

Bull-pucky? That's a new one. "Why does everyone keep referring to me as *the* cheerleader? And why won't you let Dan cohost? I think he's funny."

"See! I'm funny, Logan. Wait… I don't need you to stick up for me, cheerleader."

"Fine, I won't!"

"Good, fine!" Dan ends on a squeak.

"Will you two stop fighting?" Logan tugs on my shoulder. I hadn't realized I'd gotten so close to the mic I was almost touching it with my lips. "She's not my cohost, she's a guest. Okay, Dan?"

"Whatever, dude."

"Do you actually have something to say to her? If not, you're not going back on-air."

"Yeah, I have a butt-ton of things to say to her."

Logan sighs. "Are any of those things rated PG?"

"Yes, mister almighty Awesome Logan, one of them is."

"I'll let you stay on then. But, just so you know, I consider 'butt-ton' PG-13, so none of that either, okay?" Logan raises his eyebrows.

"I promise. No butt-tons, no donkey butts, no butts of any kind."

Logan gives Ben a thumbs-up when the piece about the play ends.

"So, we're still on the line with Dan-the-man who says he'd like to say something to Wonderful Wendy." Logan closes his eyes like he doesn't want to see what happens next. "Take it away, Dan-the-man."

"Thank you for that lead-in, Awesome Logan. You know, we should work together one day. I'm told I'm pretty funny. Anyway, I'd like to say good job, Wonderful Wendy. It takes a lot to be honest and admit you are wrong. I hope this person realizes that and accepts your apology."

Logan looks at me, mouth hanging open, and I'm sure my expression mirrors his.

I lean in. "Um, thanks."

"You're welcome. Peace out, bitches!"

Logan just shakes his head. "Thanks for that, Dan-the-man. Listeners, do you agree with what he said? Give us a call and let's discuss. Now back to the music."

He turns the mic off again. "So, what are you doing this Saturday?"

I know I must look like a goof, but I can't hold back my huge smile. "I don't have any plans."

"Do you want to hang out?"

"Like a date?"

He pushes his glasses up on his nose with the knuckle of his forefinger. The little gesture is so…him. I wish he'd wear glasses all the time. Honestly, I just want to pull him under the desk and kiss him silly. What would happen to those glasses if I just laid one on him right now? Would it be uncomfortable? Would they get fogged up? Would he whip them off Clark Kent style, revealing the hero behind the disguise?

"Yeah, sure. Maybe I can pick you up and we can get lunch?" He shrugs and pulls at the edging of the table which is close to falling off completely.

"Sounds good. That way, you can meet my parents."

His hand jerks and rips off a long chunk of flimsy wood. He tosses it into a corner of the room and turns back to me. "Um, okay. That'll be…awesome."

I laugh. "Don't worry, my parents are cool. I mean, my dad will probably want to show off all his guns, so that might be fun for you. He has them hanging up all over the house so there's always one in reach."

"Oh…really?"

"Yeah, plus, he has all these old stories he likes to tell. About his days with the Mob. You should hear all the different ways he hid the bodies. He's so creative." I look off wistfully but watch him out of the corner of my eye.

His eyes widen for a moment, and then it must dawn on him I'm kidding because he smiles. "I suppose he's where you got your fashion sense from. A hoodie and sunglasses in the middle of summer? Been taking lessons from the old man, huh?"

"Exactly." I nod. We laugh a little, possibly a lot, and then I remember what I wanted to ask him before. "What did you mean earlier with 'you're you'?"

"That? Uh, I just meant you're great, ya know? And that I… Well…" He's tripping over his words. And it's so cute, but I'd really like him to finish his thought.

But of course, that's when we come back from the music break, and there's another caller.

"What's your name, caller?" Logan asks.

"Hi, A.L., it's Capri." Her voice is clearer coming through the headphones than it has been when I listened to the show at home over the radio. There's something about it that strikes me as familiar.

Logan looks up at the ceiling like he's summoning patience. "Thanks for calling in again, Capri. So, what's your stance on Wonderful Wendy's situation?"

"If you ask me, I don't see why you guys are, like, proud of this girl. The fact that she's trying to be all 'poor me' is really lame. She shouldn't have screwed up in the first place."

Geez Louise, is this girl serious?

I lean in to speak before Logan does. "Hi, Capri. You're right. I shouldn't have done this thing in the first place, but I'm trying to make up for it."

"How so? You haven't even said you're sorry. You don't even know if this person will hear it if you do, and if they do hear it, how will they know it's you? You haven't given your real name? What *is* your real name, anyway?"

Man, this girl's voice sounds so familiar, but I just can't place it.

I open my mouth to speak, but Logan beats me to it. "She has said she's sorry, it just wasn't broadcast. And, the apology was accepted." He nods his head like he wants to say, "So there."

"I knew it!" Capri shrieks, and I almost throw off my headphones. "You're the one she's talking about, aren't you, A.L.? Don't listen to her, she's not good enough for you. She broke your heart once, she'll do it again. You need someone who will treat you right. Who will—"

"Well, thanks for calling in again, Capri. You're definitely one of our most faithful listeners, but we have to get back to the music now." Logan flicks the microphone's switch and makes a hurry-up gesture at Ben who is flipping through CDs at super-speed. "Music, Ben... Play the music!"

Finally, a piano begins, its melody followed by a rusty, bluesy voice.

Logan's ears take on a pink tinge. "Sorry about that. I don't know what her deal is."

"I know what her deal is—I've said it before. She has a thing for you."

"No, she doesn't. I've never met that girl in my life. I—"

"Doesn't matter." I give his knee a nudge. "I mean, who can blame her? You're Awesome Logan."

He smiles, and his eyes literally sparkle as he looks at me. Or maybe it's just the reflection of the dim light off his glasses. Either way, it makes my toes go numb, probably because all the blood has left them and gone to my cheeks.

What were we talking about again? "I like this song."

"Yeah, it's good." He stares at the mic and takes a deep breath. "So, what do you—"

Ben interrupts his question when his voice comes through the headphones. "I'm missing a CD, dude. You got it in there?"

Logan hops up. "Which one?"

As he looks for the CD, I fiddle with the spiral cord of the microphone. I can't believe he's not mad at me. Not only does he want to hang out, he's agreed to meet my parents, which is just crazy pants.

I'm daydreaming of what he'll think of them when he pops my hand, trying to stop me from tangling up the cord more than it already is. He's still flipping through CDs, so I give his shoulder a good punch, and he fakes a huge amount of pain, clutching his shoulder and almost falling out of his chair. When he finally finds the missing CD, he runs to the swinging door and tosses it to Ben.

He makes it back to his seat just in time to go on-air. "Here's another very important question for you, listeners. What awesome activity should Wonderful Wendy and I do on our date? Natchitoches isn't known for its social entertainment, so is there anything you can suggest? Give us a call, and we'll debate the possibilities."

My eyes go wide at the practically public announcement we're "a thing." He raises his brows at me in a question, like "Did I just royally screw up?"

Into the mic, I say, "Yeah, the most popular place to be in town is Wal-Mart, and that's not exactly the most romantic destination."

Throughout the rest of the show, people commend me for owning up to my mistake and apologizing. Callers make suggestions for our date, the most promising being the Alligator Park.

The show ends, and Logan walks me to my car, leaving Ben to lock up the studio. It's nice outside tonight, only a little muggy.

"So, I'll see you Saturday? Around lunchtime?" I lock my hands behind my back as I lean against my car. The urge to put a hand on his arm or run my fingers through his messy brown hair is overwhelming, but I don't want to seem needy or possessive.

He shoves his own hands in his pockets, and I wonder if he wants to keep them under control for the same reason I do. "Saturday it is. Prepare yourself for the best date of your life."

"I'm sure it'll be great."

He moves toward me, and I freeze. He's going to do it, I think. Then he grabs the handle of my car door.

I go to scoot out of the way, but he lays his other hand flat against the window on my side. There's no way I can move now that he's trapped me between him and the car.

He closes the distance between us to just a few inches. His gaze flicks from my eyes to my lips. My fingers disobey me and do what they wanted to do back at The Phoenix. I hook one into each of his jeans pockets, which brings him a tad bit closer.

He lets out a shuddering breath and moves to whisper in my ear, "Thanks for coming tonight, Mad." He presses his lips against my cheek. It's not a quick peck, but a long, soft kiss.

I seal this perfect moment away in my memory as one of those few seconds that I was blissfully happy. He opens my car door for me and tells me to be careful.

On the way home, I realize he could take me Dumpster diving and I'd still consider it the best date ever.

#16

Eric and I are done, but by the time Saturday rolls around, I've realized it's not exactly official until Eric acknowledges it, too. Which is why I want to cuss my phone from here to eternity and back.

Since I was at the radio station the other night, I've kept my phone at arm's length at all times just in case he takes a break from whatever super important stuff he's doing to call me back. But he hasn't.

And now it's Saturday and Logan will be here any second.

Maybe I should call one more time.

It rings once, twice, three times. After the fifth ring, voice mail clicks on, and I just want to scream. "Eric, please, please, please call me back," I say. "Please, please, please. It's about our ree-lay-shun-ship. Like the fact we don't have one anymore. Important, right? Call meee."

I'm hanging up when Mom steps into my room with a basket of laundry.

"So, how did Eric take the breakup?" she asks, adding another cherry to the cupcake of suck. "I take it you talked to him since you're going out with this new guy today."

"Logan is the new guy's name, and Eric seems to be taking the whole thing fine." Which is not a lie, since my breaking up with him is obviously not important enough to warrant a call back. "I think being on a beach in Florida is making it easier to handle."

When she leaves, I glare at my phone, willing it to ring.

Nothing happens.

The neighbor's dogs bark, signaling Logan's arrival. I make it downstairs just in time to watch Dad walk up to the door. My irritation over Eric's rudeness evaporates in a cloud of panic. My parents have never really met one of my boyfriends. They kind of met Eric once at a football game, but he was in game mode and wasn't very responsive.

What are they going to think of Logan? I can't think of any reason they wouldn't like him, but I could be a little biased. Don't parents always find some reason not to like the guy their daughter is dating? Plus, this is the crucial first impression moment. Will Dad be put off by Logan's messy hair? What if Logan wears the infamous porn-that's-not-porn T-shirt?

Actually, nerdy as he is, that shirt might make my dad like Logan even more.

When Dad opens the door, I see Logan went with a different look entirely. His hair is flat, although, to me, it looks barely restrained—like it wants to jut out at strange angles any second—and he's wearing a baby blue polo shirt. Did he wear glasses because I said I like them or because they make him look smart? Maybe a little bit of both.

"Hello, sir, I'm Logan Scott. I'm here to pick up Maddie." Every word is spoken precisely with a kind, clear voice.

They shake hands, Logan giving one firm up and down. "And this"—he steps to the side—"is my little sister, Vera."

"Hello, Mr. Summers, what a lovely home you have," Vera says in a practiced manner. She steps up and sticks her hand out. Her blond hair is in pigtails and each of her wrists is lined with bulky, beaded bracelets that rattle as she shakes Dad's hand.

I get a sinking feeling in my stomach. Granted, Vera is freaking adorable, but why did he bring her? There's no way I could have misunderstood him about this being a date. Right?

"Nice to meet you, Vera. Y'all come on in." Dad turns, and I catch his huge grin. He sees me standing on the bottom step, and his grin disappears like he doesn't want me to know he approves of Logan already. He's probably comparing Logan to Eric, who never even gets out of his truck when he picks me up. He just honks the horn.

"Hi, Vera," I say as we walk into the living room.

"I lost a tooth." She smiles up at me, revealing a gap where one of her front teeth should be. "The tooth fairy gave me four quarters. I'm going to use them in the claw machine today. There are these earrings with big hearts I saw last time we went to the—"

"Vera, remember what I said in the car?" Logan asks.

"Right, right, right. No telling where we are going. It's a surprise." She nods a lot.

I nudge Logan with my elbow. He grins at me, and those pure blue eyes twinkle mischievously. An unexpected giggle escapes my mouth. From what Vera just said, it sounds like he actually put a lot of thought into this date—if it's still a date—which is unheard of when it comes to the guys I hang out with. It's always the same thing with them: a movie and fast food, or just driving around on a Saturday night, looking for parties.

Dad plops down in his extremely worn and extremely smelly La-Z-Boy recliner, TV remote in hand. Mom has begged him a million times to let her buy him a new chair, but he never gives in. "So, Logan Scott, huh? I don't know any Scotts around here."

Logan sits on the couch in the spot closest to Dad. "We're from Arkansas. We just moved here a few years ago. My parents own the comic shop across from the college. Maybe you've seen it?"

Dad's eyebrows rise. "I know that place. I've thought about stopping in there before. I used to love comic books when I was younger."

"We'd be happy to have you. We have tons of back issues. You could catch up on your favorites."

Mom walks in, and her eyes light up at the sight of Vera swinging her legs back and forth as she sits next to Logan on the couch.

I catch Mom up on the conversation. "This is Logan and Vera. Logan's parents own the comic shop in town, and Vera just lost a tooth."

Mom sits next to Vera. "Hello, Vera. Logan, what do you have planned for your first date?"

"It's a surprise, Mrs. Summers. But don't worry, it's nothing dangerous or illegal." Logan bumps Vera. "Right, Veer?"

Vera nods emphatically again. "It's totally awesome."

"I'd love some strawberry ice cream. How about you, Vera?" Dad leans forward to look at her. "I've heard it does wonders for lost teeth."

Her eyes almost pop out of her head. "Yes, please!"

I can't help but smile at this. Mom and Dad always wanted a third child, but it just never happened, so they make a point of spoiling every kid they come in contact with.

I tap Logan's shin with my bare foot when his sister runs off with Dad. "I just need to get my bag and shoes. You wanna see my room?"

He runs a hand through his hair, bringing it closer to the messy style I love. "Sure."

My room is pretty boring. I have a vanity with a mirror on one wall. I've shoved pictures into the mirror's frame so when I look at myself I see Terra and the rest of my friends. Thankfully, I took down the ones of Eric and me the night I called him, my attempt at being brave and deleting him from my life. It wasn't as tough to do as I expected.

Logan sits down on my bed and bounces. He looks around at the cream-colored walls. "Nice. Very…girly?"

"Thanks." I sit down next to him. There's that electricity again. That feeling of just being near him that makes goose bumps dance over my arms.

"Sorry I had to bring Vera with me. Dad is looking for new clients for his web design business, Jonah is at a friend's house, and Mom has Moira at the shop. Vera could have stayed with Mom, but she hates hanging around the shop, gets bored with it. She's not really into all that stuff. I tried to tell her no, but she started crying, and well, I'm a wuss, basically."

So this *is* a date. A rush of relief washes over me at the thought. "Don't apologize, she's so cute. And you're such a good big brother to bring her with you. My brother would never have done something like that."

It's quiet for a second. Logan plays with a tassel on one of my throw pillows. I debate how to broach this next subject.

"I…" I'm suddenly nervous about telling him about this next little piece of my soul.

"What?" he prods. When I don't answer, he reaches over and turns on my radio that I've moved from the top of my dresser to my bedside table. Of course, it's already set to the college station, which makes him smile.

I close my eyes and focus on what I'm about to reveal. "I wanted to tell you a secret. It's kind of really, really secret so you can't tell anyone. And I mean no one. If you do, be prepared for backlash."

He holds his hands up in surrender. "I promise not to tell anyone."

I take his hand and pull him over to my closet. The door to my room is open so I close us in the closet by pulling the fold out doors shut. My thought process is if someone peeks in, they won't be curious enough to check out the closet, they'll just see an empty room.

There are other benefits. Like, there's barely enough room for us both to fit inside, so we're pressed against each other. Which isn't such a bad thing, in my opinion. I pull the chain above us to turn on the light. "See that stack of sweaters?" I swallow hard and glance above us at the top shelf.

He doesn't take his eyes off mine as he nods.

"Put your hand under the third one."

Again, he doesn't look away as he reaches for the sweaters over and behind my head, which just means he has to lean even more into me. I don't back away because, honestly, this is amazing, having him this close after those couple of days of not seeing him. The smell of his cologne or soap or whatever it is fills the tiny space as he makes a cute effort to put his lips closer to mine. My tongue darts out of its own volition to wet my suddenly dry lips.

I reposition my feet so I can lean closer to him, but wind up tripping over one of the pair of shoes on the floor. I stumble into him, and his arms wrap around my waist, steadying me.

The spell is broken as I curse the bottom of my closet and get my balance back. "Damn shoe!"

He laughs, reaches back up into the pile of sweaters, then gets a questioning look on his face. He pulls down the innocent-looking notebook and holds it between us.

I clear my throat. "That is really important to me. It's my—"

"You guys in there?" Vera yells from right outside the closet doors.

Logan jumps and almost drops the notebook. My arms immediately cross like I'm trying to hide something. He lets out a deep breath and pulls back the doors.

She smiles up at us. "I love ice cream."

#17

My journal sits on the console between us as we hit the bricks of Front Street. I'm having to pinch the tips of my fingers so I don't snatch it up and stuff it under my shirt. Plus, I'm still humming with nerves from that almost kiss in the closet. How many of those have to happen before the *actual* thing actually happens?

"How does Mi Pueblo sound?" Logan's voice jerks me out of my thoughts so hard I grab the door handle. Good thing it's locked or I'd be getting some face time with the Front Street bricks right now.

"Can I get some churros?" Vera asks from her booster seat in the back. There's barely enough room for her back there. A mountain of random books and boxes are piled precariously next to her.

"Sure, if Maddie wants to go there."

"Sounds great. I've never been there before."

Logan expertly parallel parks on Front Street across from the restaurant, which makes me envious. I'm the type of driver who will drive around for thirty minutes just to find a spot I can pull into easily.

We each grab one of Vera's hands before we all jog across the street and go through the glass door of the small Mexican restaurant. Immediately, the smell of foreign spices and fried things hits me, and I'm suddenly starving. The place seems to be designed to make the customer happy. The walls are the color of pancake batter, and the floors are covered in ceramic tile with a Spanish flowery pattern.

Vera runs to the bathroom, and Logan and I sit across from each other at a table that gives us a wonderful view of the river.

"So, go on," he says. "Spill it. What's the deal with the notebook?"

I stare out at Cane River and hope he doesn't think I'm crazy. Then again, that ship has probably already sailed. "It's just this kind of…journal."

"Like your diary?" He sounds a little shocked. Bye-bye, crazy ship.

"Not really. It has to do with comics and—"

The waitress, a girl I'm pretty sure goes to our school, comes over with the menus just as Vera gets back from the bathroom. "Can I get you guys some chips and salsa?"

Logan passes out the menus. "Please, Corina. Thanks."

The girl leaves through the swinging doors behind the counter.

"You know her?" I ask as relaxed as possible.

"Yeah." He says this like I should know her, too. He tilts his head to the side and eyes me. "She's in our English class. And she's been the lead in the last two drama club productions."

"Oh, right, I remember." But I don't really remember. I bury my head in my menu.

"Can I make a suggestion?"

"Okay. What do you recommend?"

Logan slips the menu out of my hand and lays it on top of his and Vera's. "The monster. We could both eat off of this thing until we're full and still have leftovers."

"Sounds great."

Corina returns with some glasses of water and lemon wedges and the chips and salsa, then asks for our order.

"I'll have the kid's bean and cheese burrito and churros," Vera says.

"And we'll have the grande verde burrito." Logan rolls his Rs when he says "burrito." I love it.

"No problem." Her eyes dart from me to Logan, a smile lighting up her face. I can see why she's a drama club star. Her Latina-bombshell factor is off the charts.

I take a sip of my water as she goes to turn in our order. "So, how well do you and Corina know each other?"

He shrugs. "I do the sound stuff for the plays, so we got to hang out a little."

That's innocent enough, right? I scold myself for getting even the slightest bit jealous. Here I am, waiting for the confirmation of a breakup, and I'm concerned about this seemingly innocent girl. At that thought, I sneak a quick peek at my phone to make sure I don't have any missed calls or texts. Nothing.

Logan props his chin in his hand and gives me a far-too-innocent smile. "Why do you ask?"

I play with the stack of cardboard coasters sitting in the middle of the table. "Just curious."

"Are you sure? Because I thought I detected a hint of jealousy." I feel him tap my shoe with his. At first I think it's an accident, and then he does it again. And again. I can't believe he's playing footsie with me.

All I can do is glance up through my lashes and stick my tongue out at him. He just laughs and rests his ankle where it's touching mine.

I look around to distract myself and notice we're the only customers. This calms me a little. As much as I love being around Logan, I still wouldn't know what to do if someone saw us here. Together. "At least we have the place to ourselves."

"I guess it's nice if you look at it that way." He squeezes his lemon into his water, then stirs the drink with his straw. "This place is amazing. It should be busier than this at this time of day. I'm sure most people are at the fast food places or the chain restaurants for lunch, like always."

I can hear a hint of animosity in his voice. "Not a fan of corporations, huh?"

"Damn the man," Vera says out of the blue, and I almost choke on the sip of water I've just taken.

Logan frowns. "Veer, what have we said about that word?"

"Right, sorry. Darn the man." She looks down because of the scold, then grins at me.

"Having a mom and pop comic book shop in a small town can make one bitter," Logan says to me, running a hand through his hair again. "I don't know if it's because we're not originally from around here or if it's because people just don't care about comics these days, but it's like The Phoenix is doomed to be just another local business that had the potential to be great, but just never got the customers."

Well, that sucks. There must be some way to fix it, though. "Could it be because of advertising? Not to be rude or anything, but I hardly ever see ads for you guys."

"Could be that. But it's hard to pay for billboards when you're hardly paying the rent. Anyway, I shouldn't have brought it up. Let's not get into it. Not today." Logan looks at me wistfully.

Corina comes back with a big tray of food. Vera doesn't waste any time picking up one of the fried churros and dipping it into the cup of icing they came with. Our burrito is the last plate put on the table. Logan wasn't lying—the thing is huge, the size of one of my Dad's work boots, and it smells delicious. The stuffed-to-its-limit burrito sits in a pool of green sauce, steaming.

Logan picks up his fork and knife like he's about to dig into Thanksgiving dinner and begins to cut it into edible bites. I stab a piece with my fork, and so does he. He raises his eyebrow as we both take a bite. Again, he was right. This is so mouth-wateringly yummy I'd sell my pom-poms to pay for another taste.

We only finish half of "the monster" before we're both stuffed, and Logan has to request a to-go box. Like most kids, Vera finished like ten minutes ago.

"Are y'all done yet?" she asks for the hundredth time in the past five minutes.

"I think so," Logan says.

She bounces in her seat. "Yay! Can we go to the—"

Logan puts a finger to his lips. "Right, right." She nods her head. "It's a surprise."

• • •

We've left the bricks of Front Street behind and passed Logan's house. Now I'm very curious about what he has planned because there's nothing out this way except for a place that sells mobile homes and an animal hospital. We pass both of those things and keep going.

If she wasn't strapped in, I'm sure Vera would be bouncing off the windows right now. "Are we there yet?" Classic kid question.

Logan glances at her in his rearview mirror. "Almost."

It isn't until we turn into the gravel parking lot that I realize what Logan has in store for our first date.

"I love bowling!" I shout and begin bouncing just like Vera. "I haven't been here in forever. Can we play air hockey? I rule at air hockey, just so you know."

Logan turns off the car. "We'll see about that." He leans over to open the glove compartment and tosses my comic journal in it.

I flinch. Just a little.

When we walk in, all those familiar noises hit me at once. The beeps and crashes of the arcade machines collide with the smash of someone taking out at least seven pins. The scents of beer, nachos, and bowling ball wax meld into this one smell that, if it were a perfume, would be called Eau de Gutterball.

We rent a lane from a lady with big, almost white-blond hair and electric blue eye shadow, whose name tag says Barbie, then head over to the bowling balls. Vera is way more interested in trying to get her heart earrings from the claw machine so she darts over to it.

"Stay where I can see you, Veer!" Logan yells after her.

After picking out the perfect bowling balls (mine is pink and swirly, his is shiny and black), we set up at our lane. I take off my flip-flops and pause. No socks. Do they sell socks here? Is there a stocking vending machine somewhere?

I'm still staring at my pearly-pink painted toenails when Logan says, "I brought socks, just left them in the car. Could you, um…" He trails off and looks over at Vera.

I smile up at him. "I'll go see if I can help her get those earrings."

He sighs out the word, "Thanks," then says, "I'll be right back."

When I walk up behind her, Vera growls at the metal claw as it opens to drop absolutely nothing down the slot.

"Did you get 'em yet?" I ask.

"No." She mashes a quarter into the machine and presses the forward arrow button. "I only have two quarters left after this… one…and…I almost have them!" The claw clamps down on the clear plastic egg that holds the earrings, but it's not dead on so the egg slips out of its grasp. "Awww, man, this thing is cheating." Her forehead drops to the glass as she watches the claw come back empty handed again.

"I have a trick for this. It's better if you have a buddy watching from the side. I'll stand over here and tell you when to stop going forward, and then you move it left or right."

I have to drape myself over the jukebox next to the claw game in order to get a good view from the side. We almost get it on the next try, but the egg is just slightly out of line with the claw. It shoots over, putting itself in a prime spot for grabbing; wedged in a stuffed panda's arms, big end up.

"We can do this, Veer. It's perfect. Just concentrate." I plaster my face to the glass. Who cares about germs when giant sparkly heart earrings are at stake?

She takes a deep breath and drops her last coin. The claw moves forward.

"Just a little more," I say.

I catch my lip between my teeth as the claw lowers. It closes around the egg perfectly. We both gasp when the egg wobbles. It rolls to the side, through a gap in the metal prongs, and falls out of the claw. I think we've lost it and try to come up with something comforting to say to Vera, but then the egg bounces off the glass at an angle and careens down the winner shoot.

I jump up and down and squeal as Vera dives for the earrings, shouting, "Yes! Yes! Yes!" the whole time.

"Well, that was spectacular," Logan says from behind us. "Give me a high five, Veer." He holds his hand up high so she has to hop up to slap it. He holds his hand up to me, and I place my own against it. He laces his fingers with mine. "You're cute, you know that?"

Later, when I'm lying in bed going over the day's events, I'll probably think of tons of different perfect responses to this, but right now, all I can think of is, "Thanks."

We go back to our lane. Vera takes a seat so she can spend some time with her new earrings, and Logan hands me a pair of socks. They're a pair of his soccer socks so when I put them on, the heels are almost sitting on the back of my calves, and they come up to the middle of my knees.

He chuckles. "Sorry. I guess I could have gotten some of Mom's."

"Don't worry, I like them. Could be another one of my new fashion trends. Two-toned bowling shoes and oversized socks are so this season, don't you think?" I pick up my ball and strike a pose.

He just continues laughing as he sets up the score board.

After a few frames, it's clear neither of us is a pro, but who cares what the score is when you get to watch a cute nerd-boy tiptoe up to the line only to almost fall every time he swings the ball? I even record the whole scene once with my phone without him knowing so I can watch it anytime I want.

After about an hour of this, Vera says she's thirsty, so Logan goes to the concession stand for some drinks.

While he's gone, I check out the other bowlers. A family a few lanes over look like they're having fun, laughing, and making bets on who will get the next strike. A small group of college guys are playing pool in the enclosed arcade area. Another smiling family steps up to Barbie to rent a lane.

That's weird. The mother of the family looks just like Terra's mom. And how odd is it that the daughter has curly hair just like Terra… Oh crap. I dive down in my seat.

It can't be. There is absolutely no possible way Terra and her family would walk into this bowling alley, on this day, at this particular time. Is there?

I peek over my shoulder and end up staring at a cup of brown soda with a straw.

"Here you go." Logan hands Vera and me our drinks.

I take a sip and try to find the Terra doppelganger again. The family is setting up five lanes over. The girl's back is to me as she switches her shoes.

"Maddie, you okay?" He sits next to me and nudges me with his elbow.

"Yeah, I'm… You know what, I'm getting a little worn out. I thought maybe we could go over some LARP of Ages stuff. Maybe at The Phoenix?" I say, hopefully in a very I'm-not-trying-to-avoid-being-seen-with-you way.

I glance over my shoulder at the girl just as she whisks her hair into a clippy in a very familiar fashion. There's no doubt in my mind that's Terra now. I've seen her do that move a million times. Not to mention I've actually borrowed that exact clippy a million times at cheer practice.

I don't know why I'm freaking out. Terra's my best friend. My Soul-Sister. If anyone will accept the real me, it should be her, right?

But then I realize it's not the real me I'm worried about— it's her seeing me here with Logan. I haven't told her about any of this, mostly because I've been too busy avoiding her calls so I don't have to explain what I've been doing. Seeing me with another guy she doesn't know about might make her feel like we're drifting apart. Or betrayed. What if she tells Peter about seeing me with Logan? I really, really do not want Eric to find out about Logan and me from anyone but me. Yeah, Eric and I aren't together anymore, and yeah, it's apparently no big deal to him, but finding out I dumped him for another guy? Worse, a nerd boy of the highest order?

Breathing feels impossible. Oh, what a tangled web of suck

I have weaved.

"Sure, we can do that, but I know what you're trying to do here." He stands and stares down at me. "Using me for my stockroom full of comics, huh? Shame on you."

Relieved that he, at least, doesn't have a clue what's going on, I focus on breathing normally and try to kick his shin, but he easily dodges my foot.

"Just kidding, just kidding! No need for physical harm." He winks at me.

I slip out of my shoes and shove my feet into my flip-flops, socks still on. "I'll go pay for our games." I snatch up his shoes and head to the counter. He calls after me that he wants to pay, but I just keep going.

"Have a good time, hon?" Barbie asks.

I nod as I keep an eye on Terra. "A blast."

Suddenly, she glances over her shoulder like she can feel me watching. We make eye contact for about a nano-second. I see her eyes widen right before I duck down behind the counter. Crap!

"That'll be fifteen fifty, hon," Barbie says from above me. I stretch my arm up to hand her a twenty from my purse, but she's glancing around with a confused look on her face. I tap my hand on the counter to get her attention.

"There you are. I thought you disappeared on me."

"Nope, I just lost a contact." I peek around the corner of the counter and see Terra standing on her plastic '70s-orange chair, trying to see over the counter. She must not have gotten a good look at me.

Logan comes around to the front of the counter. "Lose

something?"

"Uh, yeah, my contact." I tug on his pants leg, probably a little harder than necessary. "Can you help me look for it?"

He kneels down and angles his head, trying to catch the nonexistent contact's reflection.

My phone buzzes in my pocket. I peek at the text.

Terra: *Is that you?*

#18

"Found it! Let's go." I tug on Logan's shirt sleeve then kind of crab-walk/crawl toward the exit until I'm sure I'm out of Terra's line of sight.

He gives me a weird look but doesn't acknowledge my crazy behavior. "So where to now? You said you wanted to go to the shop, right?" He holds the door open for me and Vera.

"Uh." I glance over my shoulder just to be sure Terra isn't following.

And there she is standing in front of Barbie's desk, holding her phone and giving me a I-*think*-I'm-glad-to-see-you smile. I try to smile back, but it's weak, like she just caught me with my hand in the cookie jar.

Logan doesn't notice the quick exchange between Terra and me because he's keeping an eye on Vera as she crosses the parking lot. Without looking back, he reaches down and takes my hand, leading me out the door. The part of me that wants to squeal at the little gesture is quickly tucked away by the part of me that's flailing because, "Oh my God, Terra just saw me holding hands with a boy she doesn't know exists."

We climb into the car, and Logan cranks it. "I forgot about something." He digs in the glove box, then pulls something out. He holds the NerdCon pass up by the end of its purple string. It dangles there, mocking me.

The brightness of his smile makes me take the pass. "Oh… I'd forgotten, too." I laugh nervously, but he's too busy beaming to notice.

"So, the shop?" Logan asks.

"Aw, come on, do we have to?" Vera whines.

"Vera, if Maddie wants to—"

"No, it's okay," I say. "You know what, I should really be getting home."

"Are you sure? Vera really doesn't mind going to the shop, do you, Veer?"

She just huffs and rolls her eyes.

I put a hand over my stomach and grimace. "I'm not feeling so great all of a sudden, actually. Too much burrito, maybe."

He takes a breath like he's about to say something but then let's it out like he just gives up. "Okay."

We don't say much during the drive home. Even Vera is quiet, like she can feel the uncomfortable weight that has settled over us, too.

If this was an alternate timeline or maybe a galaxy far, far away, I might have the guts to tell him the truth. But this isn't. This is the galaxy where Madelyne Jean Summers is a liar and a wuss, end of story, thanks for watching, roll the credits.

I twist and untwist the purple string of the NerdCon pass as we drive through town. I'm doing it again. I'm screwing everything up. I can't let Logan believe I'm going with him to the convention. It's not right.

Dusk is coming on fast when we pull up at my house. Logan turns off the car and picks at the steering wheel where the plastic covering is peeling away.

"I can't go to the con with you," I blurt out.

He shakes his head, a mixture of disbelief and frustration written all over his face. "Why? You practically fought me for that pass and now you can't go? And what happened back there at the bowling alley? Everything was fine, and then we get in the car, and all of a sudden, you're ready to go home? I just don't get it, Maddie."

"Nothing happened. I had a really good time. I just... I promised to do something else that night and forgot about it. Really."

"It's fine." He crosses his arms and flops back in his seat. "Maybe next year."

"Yeah, next year." I nod so fast, my head kind of hurts. "I'm totally going next year."

I throw my purse strap over my shoulder and tell Vera bye, then turn to Logan. I want to hug him or kiss him on the cheek or something, but he looks like he's about to ask more questions I don't want to answer, so I settle for, "Bye, Logan. Thanks for today."

I scramble out of the car and go inside. As I watch him drive away through the screen door, I realize I'm still wearing his socks.

Maybe I'll give them a home with the Phoenix bag. Then I smack my forehead because I don't have the bag anymore. It's currently in my notebook which Logan has.

In all my giddiness over the date and the disaster of seeing Terra, I forgot that the most damning evidence of my secret identity now resides in the glove box of a boy who may or may not hate my guts after how crappy I acted on our first date.

At that thought, I turn and stomp up the stairs. Mom is at the top, wanting to know how the date went.

"Fine," I say pitifully. I can't even muster the energy to lie convincingly anymore.

I go in my room and close the door. Leaning against it, I let my head fall back and stare at my popcorn ceiling. Terra's going to be mad when she figures out what she saw. Logan is probably already mad. Eric's going to freak out when he finds out who I dumped him for.

Crappity-crap-crap.

#19

The next morning as I lie in bed, I tell myself this is all for the best, really. I couldn't continue to indulge my nerdy fantasies. What was I thinking? At least now Logan has to realize I'm not worth it. I'm going to do the right thing. I'm going to leave him alone, go back to my life of secrets—but even those secrets are tainted now. How will I ever be able to look at another comic book without thinking of him?

Then, there's the whole Terra thing. By now, she has to know something is going on. What kind of best friend ignores the other friend when she's standing right there, smiling, and keeps her out of the loop when she starts seeing a new guy? That's the kind of thing I'm supposed to be excited about telling Terra. I'm supposed to dash over to her house and be all giggly about it. Maybe I should call her and try to explain. But what would I say? How do I answer all her questions?

With lies, most likely. I'm fed up with lies.

I toss and turn, punch my pillow, scream into it, and dash away tears for two hours before finally deciding to roll out of bed. I haven't even made it to the bathroom when the house phone rings. Hope flashes through me—maybe Logan wants to talk—but then I realize it can't be him because he'd call me on my cell.

"Maddie," my mom yells from downstairs.

"Yeah?" My heart starts pounding.

"You have a phone call."

I run to Mom and Dad's room and pick up the other handset. "Got it," I call down to her as I press the on button. "Hello?"

"We need to talk, cheerleader," a guy says in a voice that is unmistakable.

"Dan?"

"Yeah, it's Dan, who the hell else did you think it was? Surely not Logan, because from what I've heard things aren't going so well in that department."

So Logan *is* mad. I knew it. All the more reason to cut ties and leave the poor guy alone. "What do you want?"

"Like I said, we need to talk. Face to face. Come on over so we can settle this."

"Um, I can't today. Maybe—"

"Oh, no you don't, you can't pull the wool over my eyes. It's like my dear old MeeMaw always says, 'You can't bullshit a bullshitter.'"

He's probably going to yell at me for messing with Logan's head. And justly so. I should do what I do best: hide. But I feel like I owe Logan more than that. If I'm in for a session of "dog the cheerleader" then I should own it.

"Fine."

"Fine. See you in an hour." He hangs up.

I throw on a T-shirt and shorts and head downstairs, hoping I'll make it out of the house and over to Dan's before anyone notices I'm gone.

"Good morning, my beautiful daughter," Mom says and I nearly jump out of my skin. "You never really told me how your date went yesterday."

"It was fine." I'm getting real tired of that word. It's a nothing word, and when people say it, it never really means what it's supposed to.

"Just fine? Where did y'all go?"

"Bowling."

"That sounds like fun. You used to love the bowling alley when you were little."

I just nod.

"And it was so nice that he came in to meet us. To be honest, I always hated that Eric never came in. Even Terra doesn't come in very often. I was starting to worry you didn't want people to meet us." She laughs, and I have to turn around so she doesn't see my cringe of guilt.

I don't want Mom to get concerned, but it's hard to put on a cheerful face. Not when Dan's at his house, waiting to rip me apart. Even though I'm making an effort to seem happy, I think she's on to me. So, naturally, I lie. "Can I go over to Terra's today? We need to finish our signs for the concert."

"Sure," she says, still watching me closely. "You guys have fun."

I'm about to get laid into by a squeaky, foul-mouthed geek. Not fun at all.

. . .

Last time I was at Dan's house, it seemed like this huge, imposing thing, but now, with its purple and yellow "Go LSU!" sign staked in the front yard, not so much. It's still the biggest house I've ever seen, but it's hard to feel intimidated by it when there's a multitude of wind chimes twinkling in the breeze.

I walk up to the medieval-looking front door and debate what to do. There's a metal knocker hanging from a tiger's nose, and there's a doorbell. I choose the knocker because when will I ever again get to use a tiger's nose ring to announce my presence?

Dan opens the door a few seconds later and walks back into the house. No "Thanks for coming over," or, "I hate you because you were mean to my best friend."

"Look, Dan, whatever you want to say just—"

He cuts me off by holding up a hand. "Don't say another word. First we shoot each other. Then we talk." He waves a hand for me to follow. But I don't have a tendency to run after people who threaten me with violence, so I turn around and head back down the steps. "I didn't mean literally, dumbass," he yells from inside.

I look up at the sky and pray for patience before following him.

Inside, Dan stands on a winding staircase to my left, and in front of me is a uniquely decorated living room. A deer's head is mounted over the brick fireplace. A bear in an I'm-going-to-rip-your-face-off stance takes up the far corner. One wall is covered in various stuffed fish.

"Your dad likes to hunt, huh?" I ask.

"Nope. He's a taxidermist. Those are all things people requested to be done but never paid for."

"What does your mom do?" She has to be a lawyer or something considering this house.

"Watches Home Shopping Network mostly."

"I didn't realize there was so much money in taxidermy." I poke the bear's paw, expecting it to attack.

"My dad is one of the best. Do you know how much talent it takes to stuff a giraffe?"

I shake my head.

"About twenty thousand dollars' worth, my pom-pom-loving friend."

The pieces of the puzzle slowly fit into place. "Wait, is your dad Taxidermy Todd? *The* Taxidermy Todd?" I can't believe it. Everyone knows Taxidermy Todd in Natchitoches. He's the hometown boy who made it big.

"Uh, yeah." He shakes his head. "You really don't pay attention to things outside your own little world, do you?"

At first I want to deny it. But then I think of not remembering Corina at the restaurant and I have to own up to the fact that I really haven't been paying attention to anyone else. But I'll only admit it to myself. No need to give Dan more ammo.

I follow him upstairs to his room, which is about three times the size of my own. The walls are papered with random posters featuring anime characters and superheroes, and apparently, the guy really has a thing for Natalie Portman. On the wall across from his bed, there's a big flat screen. Beneath it is an array of almost every gaming system I've ever heard of along with stacks and stacks of games.

Dan sits on one of the two black beanbag chairs in front of the TV and picks up a controller. The screen clicks on, and the words "Shoot Your Face!!!" splash across it in bloody letters.

I sit in the other beanbag chair. "You know, I've heard these games can warp your mind."

"That's crap. I'm a well-adjusted teenager. Believe me, my parents had me tested. Now, pick up that controller and let's do this."

He tries to show me what all the buttons do on the controller, but the only ones I remember are the right trigger fires my weapon and Y reloads. I scroll through the different characters, but of course, there isn't one woman. Finally, I settle on the biggest, burliest guy. He has a blond Mohawk and is missing both front teeth. I name him Bob.

"I'm on the green team, and you're on the red team," Dan says as a grenade blinks in the middle of the screen, telling us the game is loading.

"That doesn't sound fair. Red isn't really a color that's easy to camouflage. Can't I be on the—" Before I can finish, the game starts, and Dan kills Bob immediately. "Hey! I wasn't ready!" I tap random buttons to come back to life.

"Shoot Your Face does not wait for the whiny, cheerleader."

"Stop calling me that," I say just as my character explodes again. "Give me a chance to get used to this, at least." Dying twice in a row is driving my competitive spirit crazy.

"I didn't do that. You blew yourself up with a grenade."

"How could I do that? I don't even know which button throws a grenade."

"Obviously you don't, because you didn't throw it, you held onto that sucker. Bam!"

"Stop killing me!"

"But that's the whole point of the game."

After a while, I start to get the hang of things. Bob dodges and weaves, rolls and ducks. Dan talks a lot of smack, but at least he's not treating me like a stupid girl. It takes me two hours before I finally get Dan's guy.

I jump up and start doing a happy dance. "Yes! I got you! Bob is the man!"

Dan drops his controller and flops back in his chair. "Thank God. That took forever."

"Let's go again." I expertly scroll through Bob's weapons, arming him with a flame thrower.

"Maybe later, I'm thirsty." He rolls out of his chair and onto the floor, then hops up and leaves the room.

I catch up to him on the stairs. "But I was just getting good. Come on."

"All shooting faces and no fluids makes Dan a very dull boy. You want some sweet tea?"

The kitchen is huge, of course. I take a seat at one of the fifties-style, red bar stools behind the granite-topped island. Dan fixes a couple of glasses of tea with plenty of ice.

He sits down two bar stools away. "So, feel any better? I've found Shoot Your Face is a perfectly healthy outlet for teenage angst."

"Who said I was feeling angsty?"

"I figured you wouldn't be very happy after how your date went yesterday."

"What are you talking about?"

"Logan seems to think you had a horrible time. And I can understand why because, 'She turned down NerdCon and doesn't want to see me again.' That's how he put it."

This is not exactly the person with whom I want to discuss my love life, but who else do I have at this point? "I had a great time. It's just… There's other stuff going on with me. It's all confusing and stupid, and I just don't know what to do anymore."

"Aw, poor cheerleader. Listen, I didn't call you over here to soothe your aching bloomers. I called you over here because I want Logan to be happy. He deserves it. If it means getting the girl he's been hardcore pining after, then damn it, I'm going to make that happen."

My heart melts a little. "He's been 'pining' for me?"

"You *are* oblivious, aren't you? I guess I can't really be pissed at you. Logan never had the balls to say anything to you. You kind of fell into his lap at the shop. He couldn't freakin' believe it. It was like the kid was getting a BB gun for Christmas when you walked in there."

"So, he did tell you before I ran into you at the shop?" Why am I not surprised?

"Of course he did. He couldn't keep that a secret. But it doesn't matter now because you're screwing all this up. And I'd bet my life-size Queen Amidala poster that Kelsey is with him right now, healing his wounds. The girl has a way of getting under Logan's skin, and I heard her talking to her crew of Goth fairies at the game the other night after y'all left. She's after him again, and I have to admit, that chick knows how to get what she wants. She might not get it fairly, but what's the saying? All is donkey balls in love and war?"

"All is fair in love and war. Why do you think she's after him again? What did she say?"

"What does it matter? It's not like you're going to do anything about it, are you? You won't even go to NerdCon with him. Which is a travesty, by the way. I mean, who turns down a V.I.P. pass to NerdCon? Not that I'm complaining. I'll appreciate it more than you would anyway."

Is he baiting me? Getting me all riled up, basically calling me a coward, so maybe I'll run to Logan?

I don't know if he's crafty or if he's just a jerk, but it's working.

"I wanted to go. But I made important plans for that day I can't bail on. And he wouldn't listen to me even if I did go over to the shop. I had my chance." I try not to picture Kelsey dressed as a dark fairy, hanging on Logan's arm with that sneer on her face.

"See, here is where my knowing him like I know the Star Wars prequels comes in handy. You are, like, his dream girl. If you go explain, be honest about all this 'stuff' or whatever that's going on with you, he'll get over it. I know it."

"I just can't, okay? I don't want to hurt him anymore." I head back toward the stairs to go up to Dan's room for my flip-flops and phone.

"So Kelsey was right when she said you don't really like him? That you're just using him to make your boyfriend jealous?"

I pause, one foot on the bottom step, and I can feel my cheeks heat up.

I knew it. The dreaded ex was badmouthing me for no good

reason. While I was standing there in my blue tights waiting on Logan, she was slandering my good name. And I don't like it.

#20

She doesn't deserve him, and if I'm honest with myself, neither do I. But I'm not going down without a fight. It's funny what one snotty, evil fairy and an overbearing, foul-mouthed dwarf can incite in me.

My phone beeps when I pick it up. Eric called while I was downstairs. Seeing this makes my heart plummet. Terra must have told Peter, and now Eric's sitting up and paying attention to the fact that he was dumped for another guy. The last thing I want to do right now is to talk to him, but I'm tired of all of this.

So, I call him back.

"Hey, babe. I'm back in town, just about to head over to Mes Amis. Want to have lunch?"

My mouth opens and closes a few times. Lunch? Why can't we do this over the phone? Heck, I've already taken care of the messy part. All he needs to say is, "I understand, Maddie. You like this nerd boy better than you like me. Can we still be friends?" Not like that'll happen. He probably wants to yell at me for embarrassing him in front of Peter. I can handle it, though. Once this is over, we can go about our lives until school starts back up, and everything will go back to normal.

And if I'm extremely lucky, normal for me might—fingers crossed—include Logan.

"Sounds great," I lie. "See you in a bit."

I hang up and turn around to leave, but Dan blocks the doorway with his arms crossed.

"Listen," he says in a low, serious voice I never imagined he was capable of. "Logan is a really good guy. He has a lot on his shoulders with the shop going belly up and his brother and sisters and his parents doing everything in their power just to make ends meet." He takes a deep breath and looks down. "If you're not serious about him, if you don't like him as much as he likes you, if you can't be honest with him, then don't even bother, okay? The guy has been practically in love with you ever since ninth grade. It would totally destroy his existence if, you know, you ended up not... Well, you know."

"Really?" I know this is not the earth-shattering proclamation of love Dan hopes to hear from me, but it's all I can say. The idea of Logan pining over me was shocking enough, but to find out it's been even longer is freaking me out. Ninth grade is before I started keeping an eye on him because of his silly, porn-that's-not-porn shirt and his fraying laces.

"Yeah, man, really." He steps aside. "So don't jerk him around, okay?"

Dan and I have our own moment then. Our goals are the

same. I think he realizes this when I look at him and nod my head because he pounds his chest with a closed fist and says, "Go get him, elf."

. . .

On the way to Mes Amis, I run through what I'm going to say to Eric, but I keep coming up with the same old, tired lines.

It's not you, it's me.

I don't deserve you.

I've been lying to everyone ever since the seventh grade and can't live with myself anymore. Oh, and I've met someone else, and I pick him over you.

Blah, blah, blah.

When I pull into the Mes Amis parking lot, I still haven't decided what I'm going to say. I get out of the car and redo my ponytail as I stare at The Phoenix's lot. There's one car: a black VW Beetle, one of the new ones, with a Hello Kitty doll hanging by a noose from the rearview mirror. I frown. Now, who would hate something so adorable that much?

I get the answer to my question when the bell over The Phoenix's door rings and out steps Kelsey. She doesn't look much different from the last time I saw her. She's still dressed in black, black, black, except her wings are missing. She really does pull off the mysterious, dark look well. Her every movement seems effortless and focused as she walks over to the Beetle, opens the door, and leans over the driver's seat to dig in the console.

Images flash through my mind. Her spouting horrible things about me to Logan. Logan agreeing with her. Her and Logan making out in the cramped office, knocking the fully poseable Wendy action figure behind the desk where she'll gather dust.

I glance through the window of Mes Amis. Eric is seated in our usual booth, engrossed in a conversation with a hot waitress over the menu. I don't feel even a twinge of jealousy that he's already moved on. This is good. Plus, him being distracted gives me a chance to deal with the more pressing matter first.

I stroll across the grass separating the two parking lots, but before I get anywhere near the door to The Phoenix, Kelsey pulls her head out of her cute-hating-car. We make eye contact.

"If it isn't the elven princess." Her voice is venomous.

I'm not a very confrontational person so this whole "let's be mean to each other" thing is new to me. My only retort is, "That's me." I continue on to The Phoenix.

"He doesn't want to talk to you."

I try to see past the cardboard stand-up of Iron Man in the display window, but I can't get a clear view of the register counter. "Why doesn't he want to talk to me?"

"Why do you think?" She steps closer. "He sees what a fraud you are."

I sigh and put my hands on my hips. "Look, this whole showdown outside the comic shop is fun and all, but I don't have time for this." *Zing!*

She starts slapping the CD she got out of her car against her thigh.

"What's that?" I ask. "Some depressing, moody song you want him to play on his show?"

Her lips curl into a snarl, but before she can say anything else, The Phoenix's bell rings again.

Logan stands there, holding the door open. He looks back and forth between the two of us and chews on his bottom lip.

I give him my brightest smile. "Hi, Logan, can I talk to you?"

His stature goes from slumped to stiff-backed. He stares at the passing cars for a second or two. "Sure. Kelsey, could you watch the counter for me?"

She huffs, her exhaled breath rustling her straight-edged bangs. "Fine, but only for a minute. I want you to listen to this song, remember?"

I look down and grin at my feet as she passes between Logan and me.

Logan lets the door close behind her, and I follow him over to the corner of the building so we're not standing in front of the windows.

"So?" He leans against the brick wall and crosses his arms. When he does this it makes the sleeves of his T-shirt raise up a little, displaying his well-toned goalie muscles. It's distracting, but this is not the time to get all fluttery over his muscles. Not when there's an evil ex and a soon-to-be-confronted ex in the vicinity.

"I just… I'm sorry." My stomach sinks, and even I want to roll my eyes at the pitiful apology. Wow. Maybe I should have been deciding what I was going to say to Logan on my ride over here because "I'm sorry" doesn't really cut it.

"What for?"

"I don't know. Just everything. I shouldn't have—"

"Maddie? What's going on?" a deep voice asks behind me, and I squeeze my eyes shut.

This cannot be happening.

Logan pushes off the brick wall and drops his arms, his hands turning into fists.

I turn to see Eric standing there. His brows are knitted together as he looks past me. At Logan.

"Eric, can you give me a minute?"

"All right, babe. I'm hungry though."

"Wait." Logan steps closer to me. "I thought you two were over. What's he doing here?"

"Dude, back up. I'm here 'cause she's my girlfriend, and we were going to have lunch." He grabs my arm, not hard or anything, he's just trying to lead me to the restaurant. "Come on, Maddie."

"Wait, what?" Girlfriend? But the voice mail…the breakup that happened days ago. Today was just supposed to tie up all the loose ends, but maybe he thinks we're going to get back together? I try to pry myself from his grasp, but Eric won't let go. The look he gives me is totally confused.

"Let go of her!" Logan moves forward. He puts both hands flat against Eric's chest and pushes. Eric releases me and stumbles back a bit. His face goes from shocked to angry in about two seconds. Before I know what's happening, he rears back, then slams his fist into Logan's face. It sounds horrible; a wet, fleshy, smack that echoes off the brick and cement surrounding us.

Logan falls back against the wall, but he doesn't go down. He bends over, a hand against the left side of his face.

That's when I realize I'm just standing there with my mouth hanging open. I step between them with my hands raised toward Eric. He holds his fist out in front of him like he's not sure what it just did.

"Stop!" I yell, and Eric's gaze darts from Logan to me. I turn to Logan and put a hand on his back. I bend over to look into his face. At least there isn't any blood. "Are you okay?"

He jerks away from my touch and stares at me through one eye, his other still covered by his hand. His mouth is pinched into a thin line. I reach up to touch his face, but he jerks away again and starts backing toward the shop door.

"Logan, please?" I whisper.

"You've been with him this whole time, haven't you?"

The question is a knife in my gut. I stutter out some words that don't make any sense. "I… He… It's just that…"

"You lied to me. Why? You could have just told me—"

"I didn't lie. I've left voice mails." I turn to Eric and pray he backs me up. "Why didn't you call me back?"

Eric blinks. "You broke up with me?"

I can only stare at him, shock temporarily shutting down my ability to speak. Or think. I turn back to Logan to plead my case, but he just shakes his head, accusation and hurt written all over his face. Then he opens the door and disappears inside.

"What the hell, Maddie?" Eric asks.

All I can do is bury my face in my hands.

"Maddie?" he asks again.

I close my eyes, fighting back the tears that want to fall.

As I walk away, Eric just stands there in front of The Phoenix, dumbstruck. I'm almost to my car when he catches up to me.

"Maddie, wait, we need to talk."

He's right. Maybe I can just rip this off quick like a Band-Aid. "I—"

"No, let me go first." He shoves his hands in his pockets and takes a deep breath. "I met this girl in Florida. You know

I've always wanted to go to college there"—I never knew he wanted to go to college there which makes me an even worse girlfriend—"and she's going to go there too. I guess I should have told you when I realized… You know… But, I wanted to tell you in person, not over the phone. That's why I thought we could have lunch today."

"You were going to break up with me at lunch?"

"Yeah."

"You did realize I'd left you messages, right?"

"Yeah."

I tame my frustration by letting out a slow breath and counting to five in my head. "And why didn't you listen to them?"

"I don't know. I guess I felt bad, like I was cheating on you. And everything was happening so fast."

"Well, in those messages, I broke up with you."

He lets out a big guffaw. "Really? Man, that's crazy. It's weird, right? It's like that thing, what's it called?"

I sigh. "Irony?"

"Yeah. That."

I stare at him, and he stares at me for a long time. His face looks the complete opposite of how I feel, all sun-kissed and glowy. Then, I laugh. And laugh.

"Maddie?" he asks in a concerned tone. He *should* be concerned, I'm on the edge of having myself committed.

Finally, I calm down. "If I had just talked to you first, none of that would have happened."

"You mean the whole thing with that guy? Who is he anyway? Doesn't he go to school with us?"

"His name is Logan, and yes, he goes to school with us. Wait, if you were going to break up with me, why did you hit him?"

"Well, it looked like he was bugging you, and then he pushed me, and technically, you were still my girlfriend, or at least I thought so. I had to defend your honor... Or something."

"That was *not* cool, Eric. You can't just go around punching people."

He holds his hands up. "I know. I'll fix it."

I lean against my car door and look up at the sky. "I have something to tell you."

"You mean, something other than you like this other guy?"

"Yeah."

"Okay."

"I like comic books."

He's quiet for a while. I wait for his cringe of disgust.

"And?" he asks.

"And dressing up like an elf and playing video games and watching sci-fi and all that stuff."

He purses his lips and squints his eyes a little. I know this is his thinking face. "Okay."

"Okay? That's okay?"

"Sure. I like that stuff, too, although I've never dressed like an elf, but ya know, to each his own."

I'm baffled. Who is this creature before me? Where's the taunting? The promises of wedgies and stuffing me in my locker next school year?

Maybe I'm in shock. I need one of those blankets the paramedics give people who've been through a trauma. Maybe I need to lie down and elevate my feet. A long silence stretches out between us as I try to wrap my head around the idea of a tolerant Eric.

Finally, he says, "Well, okay then. So that's that, right?"

"I guess so."

He opens his arms for a hug. "Still friends?"

"Yeah, still friends."

The hug is uncomfortable, to say the least. He walks back to Mes Amis, and I stare after him, still utterly confused.

I get in my car and pull into traffic. It only takes a few seconds for everything to hit me.

I am the worst person ever.

#21

"Call me when you get there and when y'all are on your way home, okay?" Mom asks as we pull up to Terra's house.

This is going to be so uncomfortable.

Terra is waiting by her car, tapping her foot. As I approach, she throws my homemade Allison T shirt at me, then gets in the driver's seat for the quick drive over to Rayann's house. She doesn't say anything, not one word.

This doesn't bode well.

After a minute or two, I try to break the tension. "How excited are you? I'm so excited."

"Excited. Yeah." She keeps her eyes on the road as she turns down Rayann's street. "So…did you have fun bowling the other day?"

No use in denying anything now. "It was great."

She looks at me. "Really? That's all you've got to say about it? You don't return my calls or my texts, and now you're glossing over this like it isn't a big deal? Who was the guy, Mad? Is he why you haven't been talking to me?"

Great. Here we go. "No. I mean, he's just this guy I've been seeing."

"You've been seeing someone else? What about Eric?"

I'm quick to answer. This part I've rehearsed, at least. "I broke up with him a while ago. But he was too busy in Florida to listen to his voice mails so—"

Terra shrieks. "You broke up with him over voice mail?"

I hold my hands out, pleading. "Yes. I know how crappy that sounds. Believe me, I know. But he wouldn't answer his phone."

"Who is he—the new guy?"

I close my eyes. Here it is. There won't be any going back from this, but I owe Terra the truth. "Logan Scott."

"Isn't he in our English class? Isn't he the one who got expelled last year because of—"

"It wasn't porn. It was just a cartoon or something," I snap.

"Why didn't you tell me about all this?" Terra's trying to keep her hand talking under control but is losing the battle. I actually consider asking her to pull over, but we're already at Rayann's. She pulls into the driveway and jams the car into park. "Or have you forgotten that's what best friends do?"

Before I can answer her, she gets out and slams her door.

I jump out, too, and chase after her, but Rayann is waiting outside, her drama-pirate eyes trained on me. I decide to wait until Terra and I are alone to continue the conversation.

Rayann and Terra sit in the front, leaving me to sit in silence in the backseat. Once we hit the interstate, I duck down behind Rayann's seat to change my shirt. It's kind of hard to get comfortable in it because all the painted parts are stiff.

Terra and Rayann start practicing the chant that was my idea, and I try my best to memorize it since this is the first time I've heard it. After their third recitation, Rayann pipes up. "Are you getting all this, Maddie?"

"Yeah, I… I got it."

Terra glances at me over her shoulder. "Should we do it again? You know, in case you've forgotten how to cheer, too?"

Rayann's eyebrows shoot up as she looks between me and Terra. To cut off the questions I see brewing in her eyes, I quickly say, "No, no, I got it. Really."

"It's pretty awesome, right?" she asks, still watching me too closely. "It just popped into my head the other day. It's a good thing it did, too, because we didn't have anything else. I mean, we weren't even sure you'd show up, Maddie."

I glare at the back of Rayann's head. As if I need her to remind my best friend how much I suck. I put a hand on Terra's shoulder. "Terra, I—"

She cuts me off by handing Rayann an Allison CD. "Make it loud."

Okay, I can take a hint. I keep quiet, staring out at the passing wilderness as we barrel down I-49. Before I know it, we're waiting in the car line for a parking spot at the coliseum.

I trail behind Terra and Rayann as we make our way up to the ticket desk with the rest of the Allison fans. They're mostly girls the same age as us with the occasional young boy stalker-type and lots of parents who look like they'd love to be anywhere but here.

I know exactly how those parents feel.

As we find our seats, I realize how bad of an idea this was. Terra asks to trade seats with Rayann, but Rayann doesn't want to sit by me either. I feel like crap for ruining this experience for Terra, so I try to talk to her one more time.

"Terra, just let me say I'm sorry, please."

No answer. She just stares straight ahead at the empty stage.

"You're not being fair. I've been dealing with a lot of stuff lately."

"Oh really? And what? Am I supposed to feel sorry for you? You pretended like I didn't even exist the other day!"

Rayann's head whips toward us on full alert. She doesn't even try to hide her excitement. Drama pirate ahoy! "What's going on?"

"Maddie's been avoiding me for God knows what reason, though probably because she's seeing a guy she didn't tell me about. Like she doesn't trust me or something. And now she's trying to apologize, but she can't seem to think about anyone else but herself." I seriously fear for my life during her rant because she keeps throwing her hands in the air. Angry, hand-talking Terra is way more dangerous than drunk leave-a-bruise-on-your-arm-talking Terra.

Rayann gasps. "You're cheating on Eric? With who?"

"I'm not cheating," I snap. "Stay out of this, Rayann."

"Don't bite her head off. At least she talks to me. At least she knows the cheer *you* were supposed to come up with."

When the hell did Terra start sticking up for Rayann? What kind of bizarro world is this?

"You've been *avoiding* me," Terra says so quietly I almost

don't hear her. "Why, Maddie? You're my best friend." She sounds so sad I want to hug her, but she probably wouldn't let me.

I sigh. "It's just that I didn't think you'd like this new guy, is all."

"So, let me get this straight," Terra says, her eyes narrowing. "You've been avoiding me because you think I'd be so shallow as to not like this guy because of some dumb shirt?"

I open my mouth to respond, but it takes me a second. "Well, when you put it that way, it makes it sound stupid, but—"

"That's because it *is* stupid, Maddie. And that's not even the worst of it. Did you ever consider that maybe you aren't the center of the world? That maybe, just maybe, I have crap going on, too? Crap that I should be able to talk to my best friend about? But have I been able to talk to you about it? No, because you won't answer your phone or return my calls. Because apparently, you've been off committing social suicide by dumping Eric. I mean, who does junk like that? Only you, Maddie, only you."

"See, you just proved my point. It's all about popularity with you."

She rolls her eyes. "It is not! And you just proved *my* point. Out of everything I just said, the one thing you pick out is the last part, not the part about you being a selfish ass."

I have never, ever seen her like this; not when she caught Peter flirting with that sophomore, not when her mom took away her cell phone for making 829 texts in one month, not even when *Rolling Stone* trashed Allison's new album.

Rayann kind of covers her mouth and snorts at Terra's "selfish ass" comment, and maybe I'm acting like a child, but that's the last straw. I go on the defensive.

"Fine, you know what, I don't even want to be here. I shouldn't have come. I don't even like Allison Blair!"

It feels like a million faces are staring at me now. Leave it to me to go into the equivalent of a Star Wars convention and be stupid enough to say I'm actually a die-hard Trekker. Terra's face is the most surprised and hurt out of all of them, though. She's just looking at me, mouth hanging open, eyes wide.

"I don't belong here." I start gathering my stuff.

Terra's expression turns into a scowl. "Then why are you still here?"

Hearing those words makes my heart hurt. Just as I start maneuvering my way back the way we came, the lights go out, and the crowd lets out a collective cheer.

. . .

The lobby is nearly empty. I feel like a little lost puppy as I lean against a wall and try to figure out what to do next. I look in my purse for my cell, but something else catches my eye. A corner of the NerdCon pass peeks out at the bottom of my purse. I should have given it back to Logan, or at least to Dan. NerdCon is happening right now, at this very moment. I don't know if Logan is there, but after everything that just happened with Terra, I feel reckless.

I walk up to the clerk at the ticket desk. "Excuse me, I need a taxi. How does that work, exactly?"

The guy looks me over and frowns. "How old are you?"

"Eighteen."

"Okay… I could call one for you, I guess. Are you sure you're eighteen?" He picks up the phone.

"Of course, I'm sure," I say, pretending to be insulted. If I've learned anything about lying, it's that I have to make it look good.

It starts to drizzle as I stand outside and wait for the taxi. When it pulls up, it's not yellow and black like I expected, but just a normal-looking maroon grandma car. I get in the back and read the driver the address from the back of the pass.

During the drive, Terra calls a couple of times, but I don't answer. Might as well be consistent in my awful-friendness. After I pay the driver, I get out and throw on the pass. I've only taken a few steps toward the front doors of the enormous convention center when a drunk Wookie runs into me from behind. I hit the ground hard, scraping my bare knees and hands on the concrete. The big furball doesn't even say he's sorry; he just growls the Wookie growl and goes inside.

And here come the tears, right on cue. The rain is really starting to come down now, my so-called best friend just basically told me to eff off, and I'm picking out pieces of possibly vomit-encrusted grit from open wounds on my knees and palms.

Best. Night. Ever.

My phone rings. It's Mom. Crap. I forgot to call when we got to the concert.

"Where are you?" She sounds a lot more frantic than I expected. I almost always forget to do the "call me when you get there" thing. But then she says, "Terra just called and said she can't find you. That she's been all over the concert looking for you."

I'm such a jerk. I'm the worst person in the history of people. Of course my best friend would call my mom. She may hate my guts, but she still cares. "I'm… I'm fine."

"I'm going to ask you one more time, Madelyne Jean Summers, and you better not lie to me. Where. Are. You?"

I know better than to argue with that tone of voice. "I'm at NerdCon. In Shreveport."

"What? Where is that? Why… You know what, we'll talk about it when you get home. I'm calling your brother to come pick you up." She hangs up.

I find a covered bus bench, thank God, and I sit. I wonder if I'd have time to run in and find Logan, but I quickly dismiss that idea. I look like warmed-over cat crap. I don't want to be *that* girl. The damsel in distress. I don't want him to feel sorry for me.

A few minutes later, I get a text from my brother asking where I am exactly. He's going to be so pissed. When I see his little blue truck pull up, I dash over.

"Call Mom and tell her I'm here," he says through the open window. He has Dad's blue eyes like I do and the same dirty blond hair, but he has 20/20 vision which I've always been jealous of.

"Come on, Ro. Can't you do it?"

He rolls up the window and locks the door just as I try to open it.

I sigh and kick his tire. Mom picks up on the first ring. "Roland is here," I say.

"Get in the truck and come home." She hangs up. Oh man, I'm so in for it.

I hear the door locks click when I press end on my phone,

and I jump in. He doesn't say a word. He just glowers at the road ahead, not even acknowledging my presence. Considering he's been off getting a bunch of psychology degrees, I expected a bit more of an interrogation.

"Thanks," I say as we hit the on-ramp to I-49.

Again, silence. This is getting old.

"Look, I didn't ask Mom to call you, she just did. I was fine—"

"Yeah, you look fine. And by fine I mean warmed-over cat crap."

"Well, thank you very much. I really appreciate that." I cross my arms, sinking farther down into my seat.

He laughs a little. "You can't pull that wounded bird routine with me." True. He's never let me get away with being a "poor little girl." On one hand it's great because he always treats me like we're on the same level. On the other hand, it sucks because I can never get anything by him. "What the hell were you doing there? Mom said you were supposed to be at a concert. How did you end up across town?"

"I took a cab."

"Why?"

Now he wants to talk. "I don't want to talk about it. Just drive, please?"

"If you don't tell me what's going on right now, I *will* pull this truck over."

"Stop treating me like I'm a five-year-old!" I kick one of the empty fast food cups lying on the floorboard.

"Then stop acting like one!"

I go quiet for a few minutes, debating on what to tell him. It's when he pushes the brakes and starts to pull over onto the shoulder do I give up trying to think of a half truth.

"Okay! I was trying to find a guy."

He speeds up. "What guy? Eric? That's the boyfriend's name, right?" I'm surprised he remembers his name. I don't usually talk to Ro about Eric.

"No, not Eric. We're not together anymore. Logan. I was trying to find Logan."

"Who's Logan?" He waggles his eyebrows, trying to cheer me up, but that's not going to help.

"He's..." How do I explain?

In his calm, psychiatrist voice, he says, "Just start from the beginning, Maddie."

#22

I'm finishing up my tale of woe and heartache and betrayal and nerdiness right as we pull into town.

"I don't know why I wanted to find him. He probably would've just blown me off anyway." I try to detangle my finally dry hair with my fingers.

He glances at me with this weird look. Is that respect I see in his eyes? "Man, this is so weird. You're all grown up now."

I let out a little laugh. "Thanks for noticing." I should have known talking to him would ease my mind, even if it's only slightly.

"So, what are you going to do?" he asks.

"I have no idea." Saying those words makes me feel defeated all over again, though.

"Number one, you need to come clean with Mom and Dad. Number two, you need to work it out with Terra. And number three, forget this guy."

"Okay, well, number one, I will be grounded for life when they realize I've been lying about where I've been going."

"You're grounded for life already because of this little stunt you pulled tonight. Might as well just confess everything at once. Believe me, I've been through this kind of stuff with them."

"True, but number two, there is no way Terra is going to forgive me. She hates me."

He sighs. "She doesn't hate you. If she hated you, she wouldn't have missed most of the concert looking for you, and she wouldn't have called Mom when she couldn't find you. She's right. You need to stop thinking about your problems and find out what's going on with her."

When did he become Yoda?

"Fine, but number three you are completely wrong about. I can't just forget about Logan. I've tried. It doesn't work."

"Are you sure? I know you're all grown up, but you're still only seventeen. There are a lot of fish in the sea," he says as we pull into the driveway.

"I know, but I really like this fish."

"I'm still confused though. Why are you hiding this part of yourself? Who cares what other people think?"

I debate on whether or not to get into this with him. I doubt he wants to be reminded of the hell on Earth he lived through back in high school. But in the end, I remember he is one of the only people in the world I can tell anything to.

"I just don't want to be treated differently. I mean, you know how crappy it can be."

We turn onto our street, and he throws me a strange look.

"What do you mean?"

"Weeeellll." I stretch the word out so maybe he'll figure it out before I have to explain it, but he doesn't. He just continues to keep that one eyebrow raised in a "WTH" manner. "You went through so much stuff in high school because you practically put up a billboard saying, 'I'm a huge geek.'"

He gasps like he takes huge offense at what I just said. "And what is wrong with being a geek?"

I roll my eyes. "You know what I mean. I don't want to have to go through that. It's just easier if people don't know about that side of me."

"Oh, yeah, looks like things have been super easy for you this far. Look, high school is hell for most people. It's one of the many facts of life. But I had friends. I was happy with who I was, and I'm happy with who I am now. It's seems to me you're in so much trouble not because you're a raging nerd or because you like this guy. You're in this mess because you're not being honest."

He turns the truck off and lets a few moments of silence go by before saying, "You ready?"

"As I'll ever be, I guess."

When we get inside, Mom and Dad are waiting at the dining table. The house is deathly quiet. No TV, no music. The clothes dryer isn't even on.

This is a bad sign.

Mom motions to the chair across from her. I sit, mentally preparing myself.

She and Dad stare at me. I know this technique. They're waiting for me to spill my guts. If they don't ask any specific questions, I won't know when to stop confessing.

I analyze the wood grain of the table. Might as well get this over with. "Terra and I got into a fight. I left to go to the NerdCon to find Logan. He had no idea that's what I was doing, he never asked me to come find him. In fact, he's not speaking to me right now. Eric showed up at the wrong time and apparently hadn't checked his voice mail. He thought we were still together. Logan got upset, and then Eric punched Logan. Plus, all those times when I said I was going to Terra's, I've really been with Logan. And I'm sorry and I hope we can put all this behind us."

My heart is going a mile a minute, but Mom and Dad glance at each other. Mom still looks angry, but Dad just looks confused. "Why did you lie about spending time with this kid? He seemed all right to me."

I sigh, knowing what I'm about to say won't make things any clearer for him. "Because I didn't want you guys to make a big deal about me hanging out with the guy who works at the comic shop. I thought if everyone at school knew I like comics and stuff, they wouldn't, you know, like me."

"Is that why you hide your notebook?" Mom asks. "Because I've never understood why. It's not like I don't remember you and Roland comparing notes. He'd have his out and so did you, and you two would talk for hours about that stuff."

"You've been going through my stuff?"

"Hey, missy, don't try to turn this around on me. It's not exactly hidden well. I'm the one who does all the laundry around here, remember? I thought about rearranging your closet one day, and there it was in your sweaters."

"You hid your notebook in your closet?" Ro says from

behind me. "How interesting. It's almost like you wanted Mom to find it."

I give him the stink-eye over my shoulder. "Leave me alone, Dr. Freud."

He leans forward. "By the way, have you finished another one? Did you put a list of issues in the front so you can reference them easier?"

I nod, grinning. "Yeah, you were right. That made it so much easier to find a specific—"

Dad cuts me off. "It doesn't matter. You're still grounded, and I don't think you should see this boy anymore." He stands like the discussion is over.

"Why?" Mom and I both say at the same time.

"Because he's the cause of all this, obviously."

"Logan didn't ask me to lie."

"Let's not be too hasty here, Hank. He seemed like a good kid." Mom's always been a romantic.

Dad throws his hands in the air. "Whatever, but you're still grounded." He stomps off to the living room.

"Yes, sir," I call after him.

"And no allowance for this month," Mom says.

"Yes, ma'am."

"That's it?" Ro slaps the back of my chair. "That's all you're going to do to her? If I'd done all this, you guys would have locked me in the basement."

"That's ridiculous, Roland," Mom says. "This is Louisiana, we don't have basements because of the water level."

I leave Mom and Ro to their bickering and head for the stairs. Dad is sitting on the bottom step. He rubs his forehead like he has a headache, then looks up at me. "We don't have to have our marathons anymore, if you don't want to. If you're really concerned about what the kids at school will think, then—"

"No, that's… I love the marathons. I love hanging out with you."

He smiles, then quickly goes back to his stern-dad face. "Don't do anything like that again, Maddie."

"I won't, I promise."

He stands and hugs me like he hasn't seen me in years. "It doesn't matter what you like to read, you know that, right? You're so smart, I don't see how you got this idea in your head. Who cares what other people think?"

"I know, it's just… It's high school."

"It's not just high school. People are going to judge you for all kinds of reasons for the rest of your life. Because you vote one way or the other, because you go to one school or the other, because you look a certain way. It's a fact of life: you can't make everyone happy. But you can make *you* happy." He pokes my shoulder.

"Thanks, Dad."

"You're welcome. Now, go up to your room, and you know, think about what you've done and stuff. I'm going to take some aspirin."

• • •

I've been trying to fall asleep for a good three or four hours. The house got quiet a long time ago except for the TV downstairs. I'm sure Ro passed out on the couch and forgot to turn it off.

But you can make you *happy*, my father's voice repeats over and over as I stare at my ceiling.

Have I been trying to do that all this time? Has that other part of me been trying to break through because deep down I know I'll never be happy until... Until what? Until I'm able to freely discuss who I think would win in a battle between Darth Vader and Lord Voldemort? (The answer obviously being Lord Voldemort. He'd Avada Kadavra Vader way before Vader could even think about the force choke move.)

The crazy thing—okay, maybe *one* of the crazy things—is I broke up with Eric and my house hasn't been egged or rolled by the football team. He even said he likes the same things I do. Plus, I told Terra and Rayann about Logan and last I checked, I haven't been unfriended by everyone on Facebook, even though I'd bet money Rayann has told everyone she could send a text message to. And Terra, even after I was such a bad friend to her, was still concerned enough to make sure I was okay tonight.

For a long time, I thought this hiding habit was harmless. I wasn't hurting anyone, right? After everything that's happened these past few weeks, I can admit I was wrong. I *was* hurting someone: myself. Instead of protecting myself, I've been pushing everyone I care about away. I've hidden who I am from my friends for years. I've lied to my parents about where I've been going. I've gotten so caught up, so concerned about the things I could lose, I ended up losing something really important: Logan. Because of him I've realized how amazing it can feel to be completely free. He might not know it, but that's something no one else has done, and that's priceless to me.

As I lay here in bed, an unbidden question pops into my

head: so, what am I going to do about all this?

In issue #250 of *The Super Ones*, the character Grayson was introduced. He was this shy kid who had great powers but no confidence to use them because he was an orphan who'd been picked on by the other kids at the home where he grew up. But he never lost hope. He knew one day he'd prove himself worthy.

Then, on the day he turned eighteen and left the home, he got into trouble. Baron Gravity knew Grayson had powers, and he wanted to get rid of him before Grayson could learn how to use them. But Marcus had been keeping an eye on the baron for a while, suspecting this bad guy was up to something. So when Marcus saved him, Grayson saw what he could be one day. He begged Marcus to teach him, but Marcus, being the "I don't need any help" d-bag he was back then, turned him down.

Grayson vowed to make Marcus proud, so maybe Marcus would want him by his side. He went after the baron who had gotten away in the initial battle, but he didn't know what he was doing. He got himself into even more danger and still had to be rescued by Marcus.

Even though Grayson's plan didn't go like he wanted it to, Marcus saw the potential in him and ended up taking him on as his sidekick for the rest of the series.

I don't know why this story is the one I rehash as I try to go to sleep, but a plan of my own begins to brew.

#23

I lay low for the rest of the weekend. I do my chores, I don't argue with Mom, and I absolutely, positively do not feel sorry for myself. Because feeling sorry for myself is getting really old.

Then, on Monday while Dad is at the hardware store, I approach Mom and beg her to let me go over to Terra's so I can apologize. It doesn't take much begging.

. . .

Terra's house is so normal, so unimposing with its soccer-mom minivan in the driveway, its lazy tomcat basking in the sun on the porch, and its tire swing swaying in the almost nonexistent breeze in the front yard. So why do I feel like it holds a horrible monster when I pull up to it? Why do I feel like I could get swallowed up by the sheer hate that emanates from it?

Her little brother—"little" only because he's a year younger, but he's actually taller than me—answers the door. He has the same reddish-brown hair as Terra, but it looks like his facial hair comes in redder. That mustache is seriously, epically bad.

"Hey, Jaime, nice mustache."

His hand goes to cover it so his voice is muffled when he says, "Th-th-thanks, Maddie." Poor thing has stuttered every time I've talked to him.

"Is Terra home?"

"She's in her room."

It's a weird feeling standing in front of her closed door. I don't think I've ever had to knock on it. I poise my fist, ready to tap on the door, and then I hear music. It's a song I've never heard before, a slow twinkling of a guitar and a light, shy voice. Maybe it's a new Allison song.

I knock, and the music stops. There's some rustling inside before she opens the door. When she sees me, her expression becomes so resentful I want to go hide in a corner.

"Hi. Can we talk, please?" I repeat the word "please" in my head over and over.

She frowns as she stares at me, studying my face. "Fine," she says, and I almost jump up and down.

She sits on her bed, and I close the door behind me. She stares at me some more. It's like she's taken "How to get a confession out of Maddie" lessons from my mom.

I decide I shouldn't beat around the bush. I should just come right out with. "I'm really, really sorry. I've been a horrible friend."

"You freaked me out. I was so worried. And you practically

ruined the concert." She crosses her arms.

"I know. I suck. I'm such an idiot. I was selfish and stupid. You're the best friend I've ever had. Ever, ever, ever. And I totally understand that you never want to see my stupid face again. I just wanted you to know you're the sweetest, most trustworthy person ever and wanted to thank you for being so concerned about me even though I didn't deserve it."

Terra continues to look at me, but her accusing stare is gone. It's been replaced by this blank, bored expression.

My nerves are so on edge. I'd love a relaxing Shoot Your Face! session right now.

Finally, she sighs and rolls her eyes. "You're right. You didn't deserve it…"

My spirits take a tumble at this.

"…but I forgive you." She stands. "And you owe me."

She grins and holds her hand up for a high five. We go directly into our usual greeting. The hug I give her at the end lasts a long time.

"So, it's all squashed? You don't hate me?" I say hopefully.

"Totally squashed. Let's just forget about it."

"Forget about what? I have no idea what you're talking about."

Terra's giggly laugh rings through the room, and a little piece of my world falls back into place. Soul-Sisters forever.

"So, what's been going on? What was that music I heard? Did Allison release a new single?" I ask as we flop on her bed.

"You heard that?" Her nose crinkles up.

"Yeah, it sounded pretty."

"Really? You think it's pretty?" A genuine smile takes over

her entire face.

"Yeah, what was it?"

She chews on her thumbnail for a second. "Peter broke up with me. He called from Florida."

"Oh my God. You two have been together for how long? Like eight months?"

"Yeah, well, he said we'd gotten too serious." We both make a *pfft* sound at the same time.

"I'm sorry about that. You want me to break out the brass knuckles and pay him a visit?" I hold up my fists in a boxing stance.

She nudges me with her shoulder. "It's okay, really. It was actually kind of a good thing. No, not kind of, it *was* a good thing. After that happened, I turned on that Allison tour documentary. She started talking about how she taught herself to play guitar and that the first song she wrote was about a boy she liked who didn't circle 'yes' on the note she passed him before recess." Her words rush out, her hands doing all kinds of weird little gestures. Man, I missed regular hand-talking Terra.

She hops up and starts pacing. "Then, I remembered my guitar I got for my birthday when I was in, like, fifth grade, and I thought, 'Maybe this is a sign.'" She pauses, wringing her hands.

I can only wait a second before I can't hold it in. "And?"

"And… I wrote a song." She bites her lip.

"And… Now you have to play it."

"I don't know, Maddie. It's really not—"

"Play it!"

"Okay," Without pause, she wrestles her guitar out from under her bed.

. . .

After I've called for an encore twice, I offer to take Terra out for a snow cone, knowing she can never resist one.

At the little wooden shack that seems to appear out of nowhere every summer in the Wal-mart parking lot, I order a blue raspberry cone and Terra orders a rainbow one.

Terra holds my cone while I pull back into traffic. "Where to now?"

I start to suggest my house or hers, but another place pops into my head.

Maybe I just want to beat myself up. Maybe I'm trying to hold on to every little piece of Logan I can. Either way, the aquarium is where I decide to go.

"Yay!" Terra bounces in her seat and claps her hand against her snow cone when I park.

"It's still as awesome and deserted as ever." I smile at her.

Terra opens the door and pauses for a moment, bathing in the cool air from inside. "I can't remember the last time I was here. When was it that we skipped first period?"

"I think that was right before Christmas. I've been here since then, though."

"We totally have to sign in. Do you have a pen?"

"Yeah." I take extra long digging through my purse, though, because I know what's going to be on the first page. He wouldn't let me see it then, but there's nothing stopping me now.

I open the book, and there it is. Logan's small, precise writing. *Graffin and Laowyn 4 ever.*

Terra points at the page. "Aw, that's sweet, huh? Weird names though."

My chest feels tight, the first sign I'm about to bawl my eyes out. "Yeah. So sweet. And they're cutest, weirdest names I've ever heard." My voice cracks on the last word. *4 ever* only lasted for one LARP game and a bowling date.

I can't help it. The tears come.

Terra grabs my hand. "Whoa, what's wrong?"

It's really hard to catch my breath, fight back tears, and talk at the same time. "I… That was… I'm so stupid, Terra."

She waves for me to follow her into the aquarium. "Come on, girl. Let's sit down and have a talk."

#24

The sun is shining today, and I mean really shining, like burn-your-eyelashes-off shining. This is going to be one of those summer days where no one steps away from the air conditioner unless it's a life or death situation. I hope everyone will take this into consideration later when I run around searching for people to help me in my quest. But first, I have to start with step one of the "Make Logan Not Hate Me" plan.

I sit down on my bed and flip through the phone book until I find The Phoenix.

"Thanks for calling The Phoenix, what can I do for you?" Logan's smooth voice makes my breath hitch in my throat.

I have to control the urge to ramble on with apologies and confessions. I put on my fake guy voice. "Could I speak to Martha Scott, please?"

"She's not in today. Can I take a message?" he says.

"No, I'll just try another day." I hang up. I picture him put the phone down and hunch back over the comic he's reading, just like he was the first day I walked into the shop. Except, this time there's an evil, dark fairy sitting next to him, talking smack about a certain cheerleader.

"Whatcha doing?" Mom asks from my bedroom door, bringing me back to Earth.

"Nothing. Actually, I was thinking of going over to Logan's, if that's okay."

"Could you define 'grounded' for me because I do not think it means what you think it means." She waves around a clean pair of my socks to emphasize her point.

"But, Mom, I have to fix this. I'm not going to have fun, believe me. You said, 'It's all about how you treat people,' right? Well, I have a plan to at least apologize to Logan, but you have to let me out of the house."

She looks at me for a minute. I can almost feel her mom-brain-tentacles digging through my thoughts, looking for a lie, but she's not going to find one because one isn't there.

Finally, she comes over to me and puts her hands on my shoulders. She squeezes. Hard. "All right, but you go there and nowhere else, understand?"

"Um, I might need to stop at a couple of other places, too."

She hits me square on top of the head with the socks and sighs.

• • •

Vera's face drops when she sees me at the door. She crosses her arms. "Logan's not here."

"Is your Mom?" I ask.

Martha comes around the corner and into the front entrance way of their house. "Vera, what have I told you about answering the door." She stops when she sees me, and I wonder if she's going to tell me to stay the hell away from her son. Did he tell her what happened? Did Eric actually follow through on his promise to "fix things" and come by to apologize?

A huge smile lights up her face, and I breathe a sigh of relief. "Hi, Maddie. Vera, go watch your show."

Reluctantly, Vera goes into the living room, making sure to cast a scornful glance at me behind her mother's back.

Martha holds the door open for me. "Come on in."

I follow her into the kitchen. She sits at the dining table and shoves her husband's paperwork to the end of it. I sit down across from her. Now to begin the groveling.

"I just want to say I'm so sorry about what happened to Logan. I so did not intend for—"

She holds up a staying hand. "It's all right, hon. You didn't hit Logan. Besides, Eric apologized and explained the whole thing. These kinds of things happen with men."

"So, you know about the Eric debacle?"

She nods.

"And so does Logan?"

She nods, again.

"But he still thinks I'm ashamed of him."

"You're right. That's exactly what he thinks."

I close my eyes and bite my lip.

"But that's not what's going on now, is it?" When I open my

eyes, she's smiling that familiar smile. My heart leaps into my throat.

"No, no, absolutely not. I mean, at first I was worried about my friends finding out about things, but then Logan made me realize that—"

She reaches across the table to put a soft hand on mine, halting my rambling. "I understand, hon."

I sigh out the words, "Thank you."

"But as much as I understand what's going on, Logan does not. Do you want him to?"

"Very much so. I was wondering if you could help me?" I straighten my back like I'm about to discuss a business agreement, a merger of Guy's Mom Inc. and The Potential Heartbreaker Company.

"What do you need?" I get the feeling she understands the seriousness of the situation, too, because she steeples her fingers together and props her chin on them.

"Do you have copies of the books for LARP of Ages? I need to read up on it before the next game."

Her eyes widen. "You plan on being involved in the next game?"

"Yep," I say, then check myself. "Yes, ma'am. I want… I don't know… I want to feel completely free to be me for once. I want to get used to that feeling, too, because there's no going back for me now. I don't want to go back. Logan helped me see that, and I want him to know it."

She smiles. "Then just reading those books isn't going to help much. You need someone to explain it all, to give you pointers."

"But I kind of want to surprise Logan."

"I wasn't talking about him. I know more about this game

than he'll know after another ten years." She grins mischievously. "Go up to Logan's room and get all the Ages books you see. There are about ten or fifteen. Bring them back down here, and we'll get started." She claps her hands together, rattling the multitude of bracelets on her wrists. Like mother, like daughter.

"Thank you so much, Mrs. Scott."

"Call me Martha."

My smile stays on the whole way up the stairs and down the hall until I'm standing in front of Logan's door. I push it open slowly and take a look around like he might jump out of a corner. When I'm convinced he isn't here, I try to take everything in as thoroughly as possible. His posters, his computer desk, his collection of Star Wars bobble heads. I try to burn it all onto my memory just in case this plan of mine doesn't work.

I'm almost at the bookshelf when I glance at his bedside table. There's my notebook. On top of it is a green pen. Has he been writing in my book? That has to be a good sign, right? I run over to it, but a voice from the open door stops me from snatching it up.

"Logan is mad at you," Vera says, arms still crossed.

"I know, but I want to say I'm sorry." I attempt a small smile.

"Then, why don't you just tell him?"

"Because I don't think he'll talk to me. And I want to do something that might be even better than saying sorry."

"Do you really like him?" She puts her hands on her hips.

"I really, really like him."

"Wow, that's a lot. Okay, I'll help, but only because Logan still really, really likes you, too."

"Really? Did he say that?" I know I'm asking a seven-year-old to confirm Logan's feelings are still there, but I don't know of anyone more brutally honest than a little kid.

"Yep."

"Those exact words?"

"Gah, yes! 'I really, really like her.' That's what he said when him and Dan were over here and Logan was being all mopey and Dan asked him why he was even still thinking about you. Now I know what Dan is talking about all the time. High school girls are seriously crazy."

Happiness seems to rise from my toes, seeping into every cell of my body, all the way up to my brain. "Yep. We're all bonkers."

As Vera and I carry the books downstairs, I regret not looking to see what Logan wrote in my book, but I'm not going to push my luck. I got Vera to at least be okay with me. I'm not going to risk that by rifling through her brother's belongings even if said belonging is technically mine.

We drop the stacks of books on the dining room table. Vera and I sit down and each pick out a book to flip through. I try to read from the beginning of one, but it turns out to be just a story about a fairy and a vampire who are in love. I turn a few more pages to get to the rules and stuff, but there are only descriptions of powers and how they relate to other powers. After only a couple of minutes, I'm just plain confused.

As Martha sets a pitcher of lemonade and some glasses on the table, Vera leans toward me to whisper, "This stuff is weird."

"I know, totally weird," I whisper back.

"It won't be weird when I'm done," Martha says. "You just have to look at it like an interactive movie or play. The basic plot points are already made up by the game master, and you get to figure things out. Which reminds me, what happened at the last game?"

I tell her everything about the bad things going on in town and that my character's special knowledge about other races or whatever it's called told me it's probably a dark fairy doing all of it.

When I'm finished, she stares at the ceiling for a moment before picking up the phone that's been resting on the table between us. She dials a number.

"Is Tommy there? Hello, Tommy, this is Martha. I have a player here that needs to know how many experience points she got for participating in the first game."

Tommy's answer does not make her happy. "No, two points can't be right. She's the one who found out that juicy tidbit about it being a dark fairy. I doubt anyone else had the Race Knowledge skill set." She pauses, then, "Three? Need I remind you I only order the Grimore and the Infinites comic because you can't live without it? I think five would be the correct reward for such a studious action."

Another pause. "Low blow or not, I still hold the ordering form. Besides, do you want this next game to be mind-blowing or not?" I know he's given in when she bounces in her seat and smiles. "You won't be sorry, Tommy. And expect more calls from me. I'll be needing some plot specifics if I need to run a scene." She pours some lemonade as Tommy responds. "Yes, I know I haven't done the game master thing in a while, but my membership is still valid. Don't worry, I'll be very conservative with the experience points." She winks at me then says good-bye to Tommy.

"Did you just blackmail the game master?"

She shrugs. "A girl's gotta do what a girl's gotta do."

She opens the thickest book out of both stacks and thumbs through the pages, quickly finding the spot she's looking for. She turns it around and the words "Dark Fae" stare back at me in big, bold gothic letters.

"By the way, there was something else I wanted to talk to you about." I hope she's going to like the rest of my plan.

#25

I spend the rest of the week on my bed, devouring the LARP books. I start with every section I can find about elves or the dark fae, but I'm done with those after the first day. I could probably stop there, but I don't. The whole game world is so intricate and interesting that it sucks me in.

The dwarves hate the elves—of course they do, what fantasy world is complete without that—the dark fairies hate the bright fairies, and the vampires hate the werewolves. Everyone hates the lizardmen, and everyone loves the centaurs which isn't very fair, in my opinion. Then again, the lizardmen apparently lick their own eyeballs. Whereas the centaurs grant wishes.

I also listen to Logan's Show of Awesome every night. It gets increasingly clearer he isn't exactly feeling very awesome right now. Every show is filled with super depressing music. His voice has lost its creamy quality, so he sounds more like my Aunt

Sharlene, who smokes a pack a day. He stops asking his listeners to call in with their happy stories. Instead, he requests anecdotes about "The worst girlfriend you ever had" and "What made you be a jerk today?"

Terra and I reclaim our nightly phone call schedule. If I ever push her away again, I'm going to kick my own ass.

"What are you listening to? I love that song."

"It's the college station. Logan's show is on," I say with more than a smidgen of pride.

"Hold on."

A second later, Logan's voice echoes between my radio and hers, which would normally be annoying, but gravelly voice or not, it's him. "We have a caller. Caller, we're discussing when was the last time you told someone off. Go ahead."

"Eek." I can picture her nose crinkle up. "He does not sound happy."

The caller's voice echoes just like Logan's did, but this person makes me want to clap my hands over my ears. "I know what's wrong with you, A.L. It's that girl, isn't it? The one you had on the show last week. Well, I'm not going to say I told you so."

"Hold up! I know that voice," Terra squeals.

"I know, right? It's been driving me crazy but I can't—"

Terra cuts me off. "That's Rayann."

"No, this girl's name is Capri." I pause to listen more.

"There's nothing wrong with me," Logan says.

"If you say so," Capri says, and it feels like a heavenly light of knowledge bursts through my ceiling to shine down while a choir sings in the background. Those words sound exactly as they did a couple of weeks ago when they were spoken to me.

"Oh my good gravy, it is her!" I yell into the phone.

• • •

Saturday night finally arrives. I glance over my list one more time to make sure I have everything (yes, I'm a list maker: to-do lists, shopping lists, and now, stuff-to-transform-myself-into-a-smoking-hot-elven-princess lists). I've already put my bag full of supplies in my car so I don't look like I'm hitchhiking to Texas when I say bye to Mom and Dad.

I've explained my entire plan to Mom, and even though she doesn't really understand the LARP thing, she understands the purpose of what I'm about to do, which is why she's letting me go.

After assuring Mom I'll be back before twelve, I hop in the car and head across town. When I pass The Phoenix, a nervous tension inches its way into my shoulders. My grip tightens on the steering wheel as images of what tonight holds in store flash through my mind. First, my thoughts take the path of triumph, of Logan realizing how much I care for him, of Laowyn doing everything right. But when I park in Logan's next door neighbor's driveway—they're on vacation and even though Logan should be over at Dan's getting ready for game, Martha said it's better to be safe than sorry—my thoughts do an about-face. I have to force them to calm down, to stop picturing everyone laughing at me, to stop seeing Laowyn's life points depleted.

Jonah answers the door. He's already in his sleep clothes, a T-shirt and sweats with no socks.

"She's upstairs in her room." He turns to go into the living room.

I glance in after him as I pass. Vera and Moira are cuddled up on the couch, both in frilly, pink, little-girl nightgowns.

"Hey, Maddie, you want to watch *Miss Lovey's Luminous Leggings* with us?" Vera asks.

Dear Lord, yes. Yes, I would love to do anything other than what I'm about to do.

"Sorry, I have plans. Remember?" I wink at her.

"Right, right, right. Have fun storming the castle!" She waves.

At the top of the stairs, I stand in the middle of the hall and stare at Logan's door. My comic journal seems to call my name. "Maddie, he's been writing things. Come back."

"I thought I heard someone at the door," Martha says from behind me, and I stifle a squeal. "Let's get you ready. You can use my bathroom, if you want."

Maybe it's just me, but being in Martha's bedroom feels really weird. The walls are painted a deep, hunter green and all the furniture is in a dark wood. On top of a chest of drawers on the wall next to door to the bathroom are about seven or eight large sculptures of wizards and unicorns and other mythical beings. I pause to admire them.

"I've gotten one every Christmas for the past seven years from the kids." She kind of nudges a couple of the sculptures around, repositioning them.

"Martha, how did you and Mr. Scott meet?" I've been dying to know the answer to this question ever since the day Logan first introduced me to her.

A wistful, half smile appears on her face. "I was cheering in college, and Steve was in the marching band."

"Wow, that's different. It's normally the cheerleader and the football star who get together, right?"

"I guess, but not all the time. I caught him reading *The Fellowship of the Ring* during halftime and couldn't stop myself from starting a discussion. I'm really a hobbit at heart, ya know." She giggles.

"Was that... I mean, did you guys get any flack for being together?"

"Oh, sure." She waves her hand. "People made fun of our trips to Renaissance festivals, but we didn't care. We were ourselves, and we were happy together. Still are, in fact. That's what matters. You can't spend your life being afraid of what other people think."

"That's so...brave." I picture Martha and Mr. Scott dressed in period garb. It makes me smile.

"This one's pretty." I touch a sculpture of girl that's playing some type of guitar by a river. Butterflies and birds surround her, listening to her song.

"I've dubbed her Katrina. It almost looks like she could charm anyone, doesn't it? Even the creatures of the forest."

"Must be nice." I set my overstuffed bag on the bathroom counter.

"You can't start thinking like that, Maddie. You can do this, you just need to be charming, like Katrina here. And fearless." She smiles and nods her head before closing the door.

"Do you really think the bright fairies will be up for this?" I ask as I change into Laowyn-wear.

"Absolutely, you just have to be confident. You need to be a leader."

I trade my blue jean shorts for a pair of tight black pants that make my legs look great. The blouse I picked out for tonight is silver and silky with a beaded flower on the shoulder. I slick my hair back in a high ponytail.

"Have you checked back in with Mes Amis and Mi Pueblo about tomorrow? Everything still a go?" Her voice is muffled by the door.

"Yep, they have their tents and tables ready to go." I peek my head out. "Does Logan suspect anything?"

"He knows something's happening, but I don't think he has any idea about the enormity of it. He hasn't really been interested in life here lately. Just goes to the shop, does his show, then comes home and holes up in his room." She shakes her head.

I would say "good" since he doesn't suspect anything, but it's not good he's been so depressed for these past two weeks. Although, I know how he feels. Luckily, I've had tonight's events and tomorrow's festivities to pour all my energy into.

Just as I finish applying the blue face paint, I hear Martha say, "Crap! Maddie, be quiet. Logan's home."

Crap, indeed!

I hear the front door slam, followed by angry stomps on the stairs. I open the bathroom door just as Martha goes into the hall. Thankfully, she leaves her door cracked. I tiptoe over and watch.

"Hey, honey, what are you doing home? I thought you had the game tonight?" she asks, the whole time wringing her hands behind her back.

"I'm not going." He looks disheveled, sneakers untied, dark circles under his eyes. I just want to give him a hug.

"Why not? I think you should go. It'll do you some good, get you out of this funk, maybe."

"I just don't want to, okay?" His voice rises a notch on the last word.

She follows him to his room, and the conversation gets too quiet. I press my ear to the opening and strain to hear. She says something about knowing how "it" feels. He mumbles something back. There's a long pause, and he says something else. She responds with a loud, "Good, good, you won't regret it!"

She closes his door behind her and scurries back.

"Crisis averted," she says quietly when she comes back in. Then, she lays her eyes on me, and they widen with a quick intake of breath. "You look perfect."

"Thank you."

She smiles softly. "Come on, I'll help you with the eyeliner."

"Really, I mean it, thank you. For everything. After what happened, I was surprised you wanted to help me. You'd known me for just a little while, and I hadn't exactly been the type of girl a mom wants her son involved with." I hop up on the bathroom counter.

"Honey, I've known you're a good kid since you were in ninth grade when Logan came home with that picture of his English Honors class and tacked it up on his wall. You were the cutest girl in the bunch. Then, he started moaning about how he wasn't popular, that he was gangly and goofy. We've always been close, he's always confided in me. He confided in me about you. You two took different paths, but I always knew he hadn't given up on you."

I stare at the ceiling as she draws the swirlies around my eyes and over my cheeks. Tears try to form in my eyes, but I fight them back. To think of all the time I've wasted being so secretive. I could've been so much happier.

"There, you're ready to go. Just one more thing."

After I gather up all my random costume-creating things, I follow her back into her room. She hands me a beautiful, white velvet drawstring bag. It's tied with a shiny, silver rope. Rainbow reflecting crystals dangle from the rope's ends.

"It's so pretty," I say. Understatement of the millennium. I tug it open, and it's full of silver spray-painted ping-pong balls (for all the spells I might have to hurl tonight) and a set of seven multisided dice (for all the other spells that are based on chance). Each die is embedded with a different color glitter. I immediately name them Roy G. Biv like the old anagram they taught us in grade school to help us remember all the colors of the rainbow.

"That's a new set of dice. I ordered them last week when you first came to me with this plan. I would give you my set, but everyone knows dice are fickle things. Just because they're lucky for me doesn't mean they'll work for you. Treat those right, and they'll be loyal to you forever." She grins from ear to ear as I roll the dice around in my hand, letting them catch the light and sparkle.

#26

There's an encouraging text from Terra on my phone when I park behind the last car in front of Tommy's, a.k.a. game master Sorenson's, house.

> **Terra:** *Good luck! I know you're gonna kick that evil fairy's AZZ!*

I explained everything to Terra at the aquarium, and she's totally excited about the whole thing. Her text makes me feel just a tiny bit bolder. Which means my boldness level is…a tiny bit.

For a full week, almost everything I've done has been in preparation for this moment; all those sessions with Martha, all those late nights spent reading about LARP of Ages or as those in the know call it, LoA. Now I just have to put it all to use. So, why can't I bring myself to get out of this stupid car?

Headlights shine in my rearview mirror as someone parks behind me. I scoot down in my seat and watch as a group of dark fairies pile out of Kelsey's familiar black Beetle. Or maybe they have a specific word used to describe a group, like a gaggle of geese. I'm more inclined to call them a murder, like crows. Yes, a murder of dark fairies is appropriate because goodness knows their wardrobe of black on black makes them resemble the winged creatures. Their cackling at some joke Kelsey just made sends a shiver down my spine, reminding me of that old scary movie where all the birds go crazy and attack the humans. Then again, I could be being a little overdramatic.

Thankfully, they don't notice me when they pass my car. They go inside, their tattered black wings bumping against the door frame. Just seeing her renews my courage, not that it was ever really there to begin with. I get out of my car before I can talk myself out of it. A curse escapes my lips when I notice she parked way too close to my bumper.

My high heels click on the wooden front porch as I approach the door, echoing in my mind like a countdown to detonation. Again, I open the door before I can really think about what is about to happen.

I accidentally slam the door behind me, and every head turns in my direction. My thoughts waffle for a moment as the part of my brain that's all about running and hiding screams at me to get out of here. But New Me snaps at Old Me like a master Jedi would a young Padowan who just used the force to bring the TV remote to him. I tilt my head up, channeling my inner elven princess, and head for the back door. The gazes of every creature in the game follow me.

I step into the crunchy grass, dry and dying from the heat. The ground is so lacking in moisture my heels don't sink the least bit into the dirt. I glance around as I walk to the far end of the yard. Tommy is decked out in full wizard garb, of course. When he sees me, he nods with respect. Martha has been talking with him on and off during our sessions. He's the game master so, of course, he knows what I've been up to. I return the nod.

I find Dan with the rest of his clan. Once again, I trade nods. Even if our characters don't know each other, technically, he'll still have my back if things get out of hand. A few days ago, when I was at his house to speak to his dad about sponsoring the phase two of my plan, Dan told me he wouldn't let me go down.

"Number one, Kelsey deserves it," he said, "Ever since your jock boyfriend clocked Logan—which I'm seriously pissed about, but I won't take it out on you—she's been spending every waking minute at the shop. I know she's just using him for his access to the radio waves, trying to get her boyfriend's songs played, and I'm sure Logan knows it, too, but she's trying to give him hope they might get back together one day. Number two, my character is always looking for a fight. So, it's believable he'd jump in if things got crazy."

No wonder Logan has put up with Dan's insanity for so long. Talk about fierce loyalty.

Every one of the four bright fairies turn to me with warm smiles as step I up to their circle. This is a big part of the plan. The bright fairies see the dark fairies as fallen sisters. One of the main goals in any bright fairy's life is to "return" as many dark fairies to the light as possible.

"Well met, elf," the shortest one says. Her face sparkles

with glitter powder making her look like she just stepped off a constellation. She wears a daisy chain as a headband in her white blond, pixie-cut hair, and her iridescent wings remind me of a dragonfly.

"Well met." I echo the classic fairy greeting. "I am Laowyn, and I come to you to humbly ask a favor."

When she responds with, "I'm Sha-ra," I know I've found the girl Martha wanted me to talk to. This girl's real name is Courtney, and despite her short stature and youthful appearance, I know she's twenty-two. She's been playing for five years, she attends the big convention in New Orleans every year, and her character from two years ago became the Overseer (which is kind of like a mayor) of the Natchitoches and Shreveport LoA territories. I'm intimidated, to say the least, not only because of her experience at LARP, but also—and I know this is ridiculous—because she's over the legal drinking age.

"These are my bright sisters, and we are always willing to help others as long as it is a good cause. Is this a good cause?" Her every movement is regal.

"The best," I say. Her mouth quirks up at that.

I look her in the eyes, then glance in the direction of the murder of dark fairies. Hopefully, she understands what I'm trying to say without me having to say it. Martha put it best the other day when she said, "Even if there isn't anyone near you to overhear your conversation, one never knows what powers others hold and what they notice."

Knowing all these little ins and outs of this game makes me feel so empowered. I'm a geeky badass, and I'm loving it.

"In that case," she says, "we shall help in whatever way you require as long as it does not put any of us in danger."

"None of you will even have to step foot near a battle. I just need any potions you're willing to give. Healing is something I've not yet mastered."

Considering the amount of experience points I've earned while working with Martha, I should have the healing ability, but I spent them on other powers all because I'm counting on the bright fairies' help. They're the only race that holds the knowledge it takes to create these potions.

"Could you give us a moment to discuss this?"

"Of course," I say.

I take up a spot in the shadow of a large gardenia bush on the edge of the yard. Courtney and her fairies are deep in conversation, heads together, so I take the opportunity to scan the other players, desperate to see Logan. I find him quickly. He sits in the exact same lawn chair across the yard as he did the first game. His elbows rest on his knees, his head is down, and his hands grasp the back of his neck. He hasn't even put on his makeup. I wonder if he's noticed I'm here.

Sorenson calls for everyone's attention. I stay in my shadowed spot as he gives practically the same speech he gave last time I was here. Apparently, no one else has been trying to find out what's going on with the humans in our town like I have because he gives no new information on that front. My eyes dart over to watch Kelsey as he says this. Her arms are crossed. An evil smirk is plastered on her face.

God, I hope this works.

When Sorenson finishes, the bright fairies are waiting to talk to him. I hope they're informing him that over the past couple of weeks, they've each brewed a potion. And sure enough, after a quick back and forth, Tommy reaches into his robe and pulls out some index cards. He writes something on them and gives one to each of the girls.

Courtney begins to search the crowd as they return to their spot at the end of the yard, so I step out of my shadow. Everyone from inside has crowded into the backyard. I go unnoticed as I walk by Courtney. I casually open my bag so she can discreetly slip the index cards in it. I whisper a quick, "Thank you."

#27

Just like last time, there's a long line to talk to either Sorenson or Torrak, the red-bearded dwarf. As I wait, I start to realize there are so many different layers to this game. First, there's the main storyline developed by the game masters, but beneath that, there seem to be all these little stories going on at the same time that are created by the players themselves. Like, there's a vampire under the disco ball who must have taken offense to some dwarf's dirty joke because he's now using an emotional control power to make the dwarf fall in love with the cute elf standing by the snack table.

This makes me think of my own little player-created story. I check over my shoulder to see if Logan is still in the lawn chair. He's not. I really hope he didn't decide to leave. My immediate reaction is to find Kelsey and make sure she hasn't kidnapped him and stuck him in a tall tower somewhere. When I can't find her in the crowd either, my heart really starts to pound.

By the time I get in front of Sorenson, I'm sure I've worn blisters on both my pinky toes because I've been bouncing on the balls of my feet.

"Yes, Laowyn, how may I help you?" he asks in his fake British accent.

"I need to speak with you and another, but I do not want to do it inside Sanctuary. I fear it may get heated."

Sorenson crosses his fingers and holds them up for me to see, the sign he's about to speak out of character. "Are you sure about this, Maddie? Kelsey's been doing this a lot longer than you and—"

I hold up a hand. "I'm sure."

He nods and uncrosses his fingers. "So be it. Lead me to the one you wish to speak with."

I don't tell Sorenson I don't really know where she is. He follows me inside, and, thankfully, she's right there in the kitchen. With Logan. He looks even more tired than he did earlier. Her right hand lays flat against his chest, right over his heart, and she's looking up at him, saying something. As he shakes his head no, his gaze lands on me across the room. At first, he looks relieved, even happy, but his brows quickly knit together, his mouth turning into that thin line of pissed-offness.

"Her," I point at Kelsey, "The fairy with my friend."

"You go ahead out front. I'll bring her out."

The few people inside must have noticed the exchange between Sorenson and me because they part, giving me a clear path to the front door. My feet are really hurting me now so I sit on the porch steps and slip off my killer heels. The only lights out here are the streetlamps and the occasional headlights from a passing vehicle. I walk out onto the lawn, wiggling my toes in the still-warm grass.

I try to tell myself even if this doesn't work and I don't win, Kelsey will still be outed as the bad guy. Everyone will still respect me for figuring everything out, but that's not the goal here. I don't care what everyone else thinks. I want to prove to myself I'm not a coward. That the part of me that was obsessed with hiding who I am is dead. And there's Logan, of course. I really only care what he thinks. I want him to know I'd do anything for him, even battle his ex-girlfriend to the death—or to the final hit point, as the case is.

The door opens, and out steps Kelsey, that same smug look on her face, followed by Sorenson. They're not alone, though. The word has spread that something is going down. Everyone that was inside is behind them. A commotion moves around the side of the house. I know for sure everyone expects something interesting is about to happen when Dan's voice floats to my ears.

"Aw, yeah! It's on, y'all!" I can see the silhouette of a gigantor sword raised in the air at the back of the crowd encircling me.

Kelsey stops a few feet from me and crosses her arms. "What's this about?"

"Laowyn wishes to have a word with you, Kelsey." How lame is it she used her own name for her character?

She looks at me, an eyebrow raised.

"I, Laowyn, daughter of the Trulu," I begin with a shaky voice, "accuse you of misuse of powers. In addition to this misuse, you've also tormented the people of this fine city, thereby endangering our way of life. This is a disgrace. I leave it to The

Overseer to determine your fate." I turn to Sorenson. Behind him, everyone is whispering to each other.

"Is this true, Kelsey?" he asks her.

She flips her hair, which immediately settles back into a perfect, shiny, onyx frame around her face I could never pull off. "You have got to be kidding me. You're not actually believing this child, are you, Sorenson?" Then crosses her fingers and leans in to me. "Give it up, Barbie. I'll be nice and give you a heads up: there is no way your crappy little princess character can take me on. And no one here will back you up. You should walk away. Now."

Out of the corner of my eye, I see Logan push his way to the front of the crowd. His eye is pretty much healed now. There's only a little yellow tint on his cheek. He looks from me to Kelsey to Sorenson. Fingers crossed, he says, "This is crazy. You can't let this happen, it'd ruin your storyline, right? We still have the rest of summer to play. You'd have to come up with a whole new story."

Sorenson shrugs. "Nothing I can do. Maddie's played out all the proper scenarios. It was all legit. And she got the experience points for it." He looks at Kelsey when he says that last bit.

I raise my voice so all the players can hear. "I went to the scenes of the crimes, to the people's homes who were so unjustly treated, and through a special technique, I was able to identify a unique aura signature." Announcing this to a crowd full of vamps and centaurs, especially in this very proper way of speaking, sounds crazy. It makes me feel like I'm in a period film. But it all needs to be said so no one thinks I'm lying.

I used experience points from the first game to get a special

Aura Detection ability, and then Martha and I gave Tommy a call. I told him I wanted to search the peoples' homes for a consistent aura. He told me I would find one. When I asked him which person this aura would match up with at the game tonight, he named Kelsey. It was that easy. Plus, I got a ton more experience points for doing all that.

Kelsey blinks slowly at me a few times, and then her head snaps to Sorenson. "She's obviously lying!"

"I shall determine who is lying and who is telling the truth. Laowyn, would you give me your hand so I might search your thoughts?" He holds out his hand to me. Normally, my character wouldn't want anyone picking around in her brain, but since this is the only way to prove I'm right, I don't challenge him.

He holds my hand for a long, tension-building moment, even though he already knows what his character will see.

"Laowyn speaks the truth!" He flings his arms up for maximum effect and turns to the crowd. It works. There's a collective gasp from the other players. Then the illusion is ruined when his fake beard gets caught in his watch as he lowers his arms.

Kelsey's eyes cast about as she looks from me to Sorenson, then to her murder of dark fairies. They seem to be sinking back into the crowd, unwilling to risk their necks for a law-breaker.

She and I lock eyes as Sorenson speaks. "Kelsey, if you surrender yourself to the Counsel's judgment, we might show mercy if you are repentant. If you do not comply… I don't think you will get too far. I recommend you come with me. Now."

Dead silence settles. The only noise is a truck rumbling by.

Kelsey tenses. In the next second, she draws her sword from

her back where it was hanging between her wings. It has the look of a scimitar, but is obviously made of foam then spray-painted, you guessed it, black.

"Never!" she yells, and everyone takes a few steps back.

I hear a clomp of boots behind me. "Have at thee!" Dan screams, his sword almost whacking me in the ear. Sorenson steps between Kelsey and me.

"No." I hold up a hand to Dan. I lightly touch Sorenson's shoulder. "Let me prove I belong here with you. Allow me to complete my quest."

Sorenson nods. "Your character sheet, please?" I give him my sheet from my bag. He goes over to Kelsey and asks for the same thing. She reaches into her bra and pulls out her sheet, hands it to him, then returns to her ready stance.

Sorenson goes back to the sidelines and whispers into Torrak's ear. Then he hands him something from the depths of his cloak. Torrak dashes to the sidewalk. He hops into a car parked directly in front of us, rolls down the windows, and turns on the stereo. A heavy, thumping, techno beat starts. Is that the Matrix soundtrack?

I'm unprepared, distracted by Torrak as he shuffles back to the circle, when Kelsey rushes me, sword high in the air. She tags me on the shoulder. Of course, it doesn't physically hurt, but when Sorenson yells, "Negative twenty health points from Laowyn," my jaw clenches in anguish.

With my focus fully on her, Kelsey and I begin to circle each other. Thank goodness I took off those heels.

"I know why you're really doing this," she says. "He's over you. He wouldn't touch your skanky ass if you were the last cheerleader on Earth."

Her words sting, but I didn't do all this to give up now. My hand tightens around a ping-pong ball, a.k.a. an energy bolt, in my bag. I juke to the left, and she swings, but I've already doubled back to my right. My bolt flies straight and true, bouncing off her left temple.

"Negative twenty from Kelsey," Sorenson says.

I continue around her and hit her in the back with another ball while she's still looking around for what hit her the first time.

"Another twenty from Kelsey."

"How are her hits as powerful as mine? There's no way—"

I tag her again on the arm.

"I was talking out of character! That means pause the fight, bitch." She whacks her sword on the ground.

I cross my fingers, then look at Sorenson. "But her fingers weren't crossed, right?"

Dan pipes up from behind me, "I didn't see her fingers crossed."

"Neither did I," Sorenson says. "The hit counts."

Kelsey's head whips from face to face, looking for someone to lie for her. Her gaze lands on me, that snarl of hers in rare form. I wink and uncross my fingers to arm myself with another ball.

She lunges at me, swinging at my knees, but I'm faster. I jump and manage to do a textbook toe-touch. *Thank you, cheerleading.* The crowd lets out a collective, "Whoa!"

Her momentum puts her off balance, and she almost falls. She catches herself with one hand. I take the chance to throw another ball, but amazingly, she deflects it with her sword and regains her footing.

We begin circling each other again, both of us too stubborn to be the first to look away. She charges me, randomly slashing the air. I just keep backing up, slinging ball after ball at her chest.

"That's another twenty, forty, sixty! Kelsey, stop charging!" Sorenson tries to run over to us, but trips on his ill-fitting robe.

"Pause, Kelsey, pause!" Logan's voice comes from somewhere behind me.

She doesn't stop. She keeps swinging at me. I've run out of ammo, and there's nowhere to run considering we're surrounded by people. The rules in the handbook state if a character runs out of magical ammo, the game master should pause the fight so said character can restock. That's apparently what Sorenson and Logan are trying to do, but Kelsey isn't listening.

I duck under her sword and try to sidestep around her. Maybe there are some balls on the ground nearby? She misses me as I duck but swings again and catches me in my back. Not only does she hit me with her sword, but her other forearm follows. It slams into me, knocking me to the ground.

#28

"Stop!" Sorenson yells again as he steps between us. "That last hit doesn't count, and you know it, Kelsey. She's allowed to reload on magic."

"But I hit her fair and square!" Her voice is so high I expect to see the neighborhood strays come jogging up any second.

"That was not fair, you hit her. For real, you hit her," Dan says.

The crowd begins to murmur. I hear words like "ejected" and "suspension" thrown around.

I sit up. "No. I'll take that last hit." Her not crossing her fingers was one thing, but I'll be dammed if I win the whole shebang on a technicality.

"Are you sure? A move like that is cause for ejection from—"
I don't let Sorenson finish. "I'm sure."

Something hits my arm, and I look around thinking one of

Kelsey's friends has decided to enter the fight. But it's just one of my own energy bolts lying on the grass next to me. Another one hits my leg, then another lands by my hand. The surrounding players are searching the ground for my ping-pong balls and tossing them to me. One person, the only female dwarf in the game that I've seen, actually brings me a handful.

"Kick the crap out of her," she whispers to me, then returns to the crowd.

I scoop all the balls back into my bag. I stand up and dust the grass and dirt from my clothes. Everyone applauds like I'm an injured basketball player that just got up off the court.

Kelsey stands by Sorenson, grasping and releasing the hilt of her sword. She huffs like she just ran all the way to the Hot Topic store in Alexandria.

Sorenson faces me and in his most distinguished British accent, says, "Are you prepared to continue the battle, elfling?"

I straighten my back, square my shoulders, and look from side to side at all the painted and made-up faces around me. They all seem to lean forward, eyes unblinking. There's only one person I'm looking for, though. Logan stands by Dan with the same look of disbelief as everyone else.

"Let's do this," I finally say to Tommy. "And don't call me elfling, Gandalf."

The crowd cheers as Kelsey and I face off again. Her skin has turned an apple red, which, with her black ensemble, is not a good look. Not that I can really say anything. My hair probably looks like a bird's nest complete with dead grass from my tumble on the lawn.

She snatches her character sheet from Sorenson. When she

glances over it, her frown confirms my suspicions. If I'm right, Kelsey's character should be close to incapacitation. Just one or two more hits and I'll be able to bring my plan to fruition, hopefully.

Sorenson steps back to the sidelines. "Resume!"

I wait for Kelsey to make a move. Instead of charging, she says, "I heal."

The rules state that, depending on a character's level, they can only dodge attacks while they heal. The higher the level, the shorter the amount of time they can't retaliate.

"It'll take you five seconds," Sorenson says, which means her character isn't as awesome as she'd like everyone to believe. "One one thousand..."

I throw a ball, but she's ready. She dodges easily.

"Two one thousand. Three..." The crowd joins Sorenson in counting.

This is my last chance to tag her before she heals a substantial amount of health points potentially putting me at the disadvantage. I aim at her left thigh, head toward her, and swing my arm. She darts to her right, but fails to notice I didn't actually throw the ball.

"Four one thousand..."

My arm follows her motion, and the ball still in my hand easily connects with the exposed skin on her upper arm. She screams like I really did just slam an energy bolt into her.

"You're down!" Tommy says, and the crowd hoots and jumps. Dan is shaking Logan by his jacket as he throws his head back and howls.

I look at Kelsey, and she's staring at me like I just dropped out of the sky.

I shrug and say, "Sorry," as sincerely as possible.

Once the crowd calms down, Sorenson steps up to us. "What do you want to do with your prisoner, Laowyn?"

"I cast the elven incantation Change of Heart," I declare.

"No way!" Kelsey says.

"Hold up." Logan holds out his hand to Sorenson. "Let me see her sheet. There's no way she can have that spell."

Sorenson looks at me for my permission to let Logan see my character sheet. I nod. Logan takes it and scours it.

I'm not surprised he doubts me. This specific spell is super expensive, hence why I had to get the potions from the bright fairies instead of getting the healing power. When he shakes his head in disbelief, I stand next to him and point at my experience point expenditure log.

"Did I do it right?" I ask.

His bright blue eyes lock with mine. "How..."

I lean in so close our noses are almost touching. "Ask your mom."

He blinks a few times, then gives my sheet back to Sorenson. "Looks good to me."

"Uh-uh," Kelsey says. "Let me see that thing."

"It has been approved by two game masters and another player. There's no need for you to look at it," Sorenson says.

Kelsey's mouth drops open.

Sorenson straightens my character sheet. "Now, Maddie, you do realize this spell takes health points to initiate and if you use it now, it'll kill you, so—"

I pull out the index cards from the bright fairies and shove them against Sorenson's chest.

He reads them and grins. "You sneaky little elf. All right, these potions put you at full health. You'll survive the casting, but only barely." He throws his arms up to get the chattering crowd's attention. "For those of you who aren't familiar with the incantation called Change of Heart, Maddie will need to roll seven different dice. It's extremely difficult to complete this spell because of what it does. It completely changes the target's sensibilities. If your character loves winter, after this spell, she'll love summer. If she loves order, after this spell, she'll love chaos. If she is dark, after this spell, she'll be bright."

The crowd's chattering gets louder as Sorenson explains things. I look up at Logan. He's still staring at me with a bewildered look on his face.

Sorenson continues. "This spell is not only hard to cast because it saps your health, it is considered nearly impossible because you must roll perfect on five of the seven dice."

He forgot to mention that the five dice have to be the five highest-rolling dice. I have to roll a twenty on the twenty-sided die, a twelve on the twelve-sided die, a ten on both ten-sided dice, and an eight on the eight-sided die. I don't even want to try to calculate the odds on this or my brain will explode.

"Do you have a set of dice? I think I have a spare upstairs," Sorenson says to me.

I pull out Roy G. Biv. "I have my own."

The crowd parts for Sorenson, Kelsey, Logan, and me as we head up to the porch. Tommy clears a coffee table that looks more like a Dumpster treasure than a table. I kneel down in front of it, and Kelsey pulls up a chair.

"This is never going to work, you know that, right? You're going to knock yourself out, I'll wake up before you, and chop your head off," she says.

"Not if I chop yours off first," Dan says from the steps.

I just smile and rub the dice in my hands. They click together creating a twinkling tune.

Sorenson kneels down. I can feel Logan standing above me.

"Here I go," I say.

Everything goes into slow motion when the dice fall from my fingers. Each one bounces a couple of times then rolls along the table, one after the other, their rainbow colors reflecting the dim porch light. I force myself not to watch them as they come to a stop. When the last one leaves my hand, I stand and turn around, putting me face to face with Logan.

He's not watching the outcome either. His eyes sparkle like the dice, bright and sigh-inducing. His brow is furrowed, though, making me wonder what is running through his mind. I find out soon enough. His fingertips lightly touching the sides of my neck are the only things I feel as the dice are totaled behind me. The creases between his eyebrows disappear as the smile that struck me as irresistible the first time I saw it in The Phoenix appears. I breathe in his scent, and my eyes drift shut like I just caught a whiff of hot chocolate on Christmas day. I forget where I am when his perfect boy-lips brush against mine.

Then, we kiss. We kiss like no else exists, like we were made for each other, like there's nowhere else in the entire world either one of us wants to be.

When we break apart, my heart goes into overdrive. I lean into Logan, resting my forehead against his. Somehow, my hands slipped under his jacket and are now flat against his chest. I try to pull them back, but he covers them with his own, keeping them in place. My blue face paint has transferred to his nose and cheeks making him look slightly frost-bitten.

"*Finally*," he says, voice ragged. I like this tone a lot more than his normal, smooth radio voice.

"Finally what?" My voice is just as shaky as his.

He opens his mouth to say something, but Kelsey shouts, "No freakin' way!"

Sorenson stands slowly, still staring at the table. "I can't believe it," he says in a whisper. Then he turns to the crowd, which I now realize has been deathly quiet this whole time. "Six out of seven rolled high number! The spell is complete!"

The crowd roars. People rush forward to congratulate me, shaking my hands, slapping my back.

"That was the best thing ever!" a guy vamp says, his yellow contact covered eyes wide.

"I can't believe it. You're one badass mamma-jamma," a lizard girl says as she squeezes my shoulder.

Dan shoves through the sea of people. "That was the most donkey-butt crazy shit I've ever witnessed!" He punctuates every word by bonking my head with his gigantor sword.

"Excuse us," Sha-ra says, and people hop off the porch and the steps to make room for her and her crew.

She puts a hand on Kelsey's shoulder. Kelsey looks up at her with frantic eyes, then jumps up and backs away.

"No, no, this can't be happening." She shakes her head the whole time.

"Don't be afraid, sister," Sha-ra says. "You are one of us

now. We're going to have to do something about your wardrobe, though."

As Sha-ra drags Kelsey off the porch by the arm, Kelsey searches for her murder. "Avenge me! Avenge me!"

"Uh-uh," Sorenson says. "Don't act out-of-character. She wouldn't say that now. The second the spell was cast, your character became bright. She'd be thankful for Laowyn's actions."

I cover my mouth and look around to see if Logan notices the humor in the whole scene, too, but I can't find him.

I try to wade through the crowd, searching each face for him, but every player has something to say to me.

"That took a lot of guts, elf," a broad dwarf says and claps me hard on the back.

Another vampire, this one tall with a top hat and a monocle, stops me. "You are welcome at the Critory clan's castle anytime, Lady Laowyn." I nod respectfully, trying to stay in character even though I have no idea what he's talking about.

Finally, the players start to dissipate, moving back inside or to the backyard.

I spend the next thirty minutes looking for Logan, but he's nowhere to be found.

#29

I tossed and turned all night. And I blame it all on Logan Scott and those perfect boy-lips of his. Sure, I won. I defeated the evil fairy and saved the day. I can't wait to go to the next game and be heralded as a hero. Facing Logan might be tough, though, seeing as what I did wasn't enough to save our relationship

I looked for him but never found him. He also never called. I know, because I stared at my phone most of the night, waiting. His disappearance has to mean something. Most likely, "Sorry, Maddie. He got what he came for and now he's over it."

"So, today's the big day," Mom says when I come downstairs. It is six o'clock in the morning, way too early to be wearing my scratchy, maroon and gold cheer uniform, but even though Logan isn't interested any more, I've worked too hard on this part of the plan to let it go. It's too important to me and everyone involved. So, I have to be there on time, thirty minutes from now.

"Yep." I'm surprised my sleep-deprived brain can even say that simple word.

"How'd it go last night? Did you stop the evil…what was it?"

"Dark fairy. Yes, I did. Everything went as planned." Except for the part where I was supposed to get Logan back. That went completely against the plan.

"Good, good. You know, I just love you in your uniform. You look so nice, you have such a cute figure and the bow with the ponytail is—"

"Cut it out, Mom. I don't think I can take all the gushing this early." I give her a playful love tap on the shoulder.

She returns the tap with a slight push on my arm. "Fine, be grumpy."

As I slather some raspberry jam on a slice of buttered toast, she leans against the counter and watches me with a grin.

"Stop looking at me like that," I say.

"Why?"

I take a huge bite of toast. "'Cause it's freaking me out."

"I was just thinking." She sips her coffee. "You really like this boy, don't you?"

I stare out the window into the gray morning as I chew. Do I "really like" him? Is that the right way to put it? I've only known him for the summer technically, but "really like" doesn't seem to encompass it. If you "really like" someone, do they insist on invading your every thought? Does just saying their name make goose bumps rise on your arms? Do you contemplate how many freckles your children will have?

"Yeah, I really like him."

Mom would definitely freak out if I told her how I actually feel.

• • •

When I get to The Phoenix, Martha, Vera, Jonah, and Mr. Scott are setting up tables in front of the display windows.

"Good morning, sunshine," Martha says.

"Morning," I say. Then, I'm almost knocked down when Vera runs into me and clasps her arms around me in a hug.

"This is going to be so much fun, Maddie. I can't wait to see the cheerleaders. Are you guys going to do flips and cheers and oh, a pyramid thing? Please do a pyramid thing!" Vera strings her words together. What has she eaten to be so awake this early, and where can I get some of this magical substance?

"I'll tell the girls you request a pyramid," I say.

"Veer, go help Daddy with the boxes in the back room, please," Martha says.

Vera takes off to the front door, pausing before she goes inside to attempt a hurky jump. The girl has decent form for a seven-year-old.

"Want to help me hang the banner?" Martha asks.

I'm surprised she hasn't begun interrogating me about what happened last night. I nod and pick up the large folded plastic sign from one of the tables., and stretch it out on the concrete while Martha goes to get a ladder and scan the sign for typos.

1ST ANNUAL NATCHITOCHES SMALL BUSINESS FESTIVAL

The local signage place did a great job.

It suddenly hits me how unbelievable it is that we got all this together in such a short period of time when the Mi Pueblo van pulls up. Corina hops out and opens the back doors. She waves as I walk up.

I help her pull out a cooler. "Good morning. I just wanted to say thanks for taking part in this."

"Are you kidding? My mom thinks this is a wonderful idea. She's been running around like a crazy person all week getting everything ready."

"I have not been crazy," Mrs. Garcia says as she comes around the corner of the van.

Mi Pueblo was the first business I approached other than The Phoenix with the idea of having a small business festival. Mrs. Garcia was so stoked about it, she signed up in two minutes flat. The same thing happened with pretty much every other business I went to. They didn't even mind a small percentage of all of their proceeds would go to local charities and the college's radio department. That seemed to be the cherry on the cupcake for them, in fact.

There's only so much room in The Phoenix's lot, though, so when businesses started calling Martha about reserving a spot, I went next door to Mes Amis. They offered up their lot as well. Then the problem of where people were going to park came up. Luckily, the college library across the street was more than happy to help seeing as their lot is huge.

There were also permits to be gotten and that's where Dan's dad, a.k.a. Taxidermy Todd, came into play. Without his connections in the city council, none of this would be happening.

Then it was just a matter of promotion. My cheerleading coach was all for recruiting the squad to help spread the word seeing as her partner, Sarah, reserved a spot for her bookstore. Plus, the college radio station has been broadcasting the where and when of the festival, like, every ten minutes for the past week.

Now, all I can hope for is the heat won't keep customers from coming out.

By the time Martha and I get the banner hung, things are in full swing. I hand out copies of the layout to every business so they know where to set up. Tents and tables start dotting the two parking lots. Everything is going smoothly. I couldn't ask for anything more.

Except, maybe, for a certain someone to show up.

I get a call, and I know it's Dan before I answer because he's earned himself his own ringtone: the Mario Brothers' theme song.

"We're in the back. Get your lazy ass back here and help us with this crap." He hangs up before I even say hello.

As I come around the corner to the back lot, Dan's dad steps out of his massive Suburban. I'm still slightly mesmerized by his beauty. His long, lean legs were made to wear those cowboy boots. He smiles a dazzling smile as he smooths back his longish, wavy hair and pulls on a baseball cap. I know the man is almost forty, but a girl can look. From the moment I met Mr. Garrett, I knew I was right about Dan being the type of guy who's going to get better looking as he ages.

"What do you think, Maddie?" Mr. Garrett points to his hat. It has the festival's logo, then underneath it says, "Sponsored by Garrett Taxidermy."

"It's perfect. Thanks again for your help, Mr. Garrett."

"It's no problem. This is a great thing you've thought up. And what better business to sponsor something like this than a small business that's made it big, like mine."

Dan walks out from the back of the large, black Suburban carrying a big box. "If your puny arms can handle it, why don't you help us with these T-shirts," he says.

"Someone's not a morning person."

"Bite my chunky—"

"Daniel!" Mr. Garrett yells from the alley. "What did I tell you about how to treat a lady?"

Dan just grumbles as he follows his dad.

When I go to the open back end of the Suburban, I freeze at the sight before me. Logan sits on top of one of the boxes reading a notebook. *My* notebook.

I clear my throat, and he looks up. Mr. Garrett might have dreamy eyes, but there's no competition when it comes to Logan's blue stare. He closes the notebook, drops it in a seat behind him, and opens the box he was sitting on. "I hope we sell the hell out of these things because Dan's dad bought about a million of them." He pulls out one of the festival T-shirts and hops out of the Suburban.

I notice some blue paint under his fingernail. My cheeks suddenly feel extremely hot because I know where that paint came from.

He opens another box. "And these are genius." He holds up a fan/water squirter also sporting the festival's logo.

I just nod.

We each take a box, and I follow him down the alley, questions flooding my mind. Where did he go last night? What did he mean by "finally"? Did he mean, "finally this is happening," or, "finally I can put my feelings for this girl to rest and move on," like I suspect? But when we make it to the front, I realize now is not the time.

Cars are already filling up the library parking lot. Plus, Terra and Rayann are jogging across the street.

Dan brings out a dolly, and Logan and I stack our boxes on it. I turn to Logan, hoping I might be able to get in at least one question before everything gets hectic, but he's looking at his phone.

"Ben's here. I have to go help him." He points at the alley.

"Okay," I say, even though I feel the exact opposite.

#30

"Oh my God, I'll be so glad when this is over," Rayann says as she and Terra approach, both decked out in their cheer uniforms.

"You're just going to have to deal with the heat. This is an awesome thing Maddie has put together. Who cares if your makeup runs?"

I want to hug the crap out of Terra for standing up to Rayann. Instead, we go directly into our high fives and ankle-kicks.

"This is great, Maddie. I'm so proud of you," she says.

"Is Chili's going to have a booth, I could really go for some—"

I cut Rayann off by holding up a hand. "Chili's is not exactly the right business for this event. It's called the Small Business Festival, remember?"

Once the rest of the squad shows up, we get to it. We perform every hour on the hour. By midday, Vera knows all our moves and cheers. She stands in front of us with her friends, copying our routines. It's so cute, I can hardly stand it.

We take a break, grabbing cold water bottles from our coolers, and listen to Logan over the speakers.

"Oh, I didn't even notice we had a radio station here. Thought it was just a CD player?" Rayann nods at one of the speakers. "What station is it?"

"The college station. They're getting some of the profits from today. Did you even read the flier you were supposed to have put up all over town?" I ask.

"The college radio station? As in 'Awesome Logan's Show of Awesome'? Oh my God, I love him. I listen to his show every night. I call in all the time. Is he going to be here?"

"He's here already." I grin at Terra. "In fact, there he is." I point at Logan sitting at station's table into front of the comic shop.

After realizing Capri is actually Rayann, Terra and I knew it was only a matter of time before she found out she had a crush on a nerd, but this is better than any reveal we could've come up with. Rayann frowns and tilts her head to the side like a confused poodle. "Isn't that... Wait, A.L. is Logan Scott? The porn shirt guy? I can't believe I actually asked him for his number. Yuck."

Logan spots us. I smile at him, and he waves back.

Her confused poodle-face turns to me. "Wait, are you... You're Wonderful Wendy?"

"Yep."

"But... He's such a nerd. Everyone knows it. I mean, you can't go to prom with...with...that!" She raises her voice a little too high, and the rest of the squad turns their heads to watch.

She sits on one of the coolers, apparently too stunned by my treachery to stand. I glare at her, my hand crushing the almost empty water bottle I'm holding. "You know what, Rayann? I don't give a rat's ass what you think. Or what anyone thinks, for that matter. You don't know him, and you definitely don't know me. He's the sweetest, most considerate guy ever. And if he wants to wear that 'porn shirt'—which by the way is Power Girl drawn by Adam Hughes and it's a freaking work of art—and his old sneakers to prom, I'd be proud to go with him. So, you can take your shallow self back to the pirate ship and leave us alone."

Not only is the squad watching, but a lot of other people are, too. What's awesome is that I don't even have the urge to run away and hide. I throw my shoulders back and don't break eye contact with Rayann. There's a snicker behind me I quickly recognize as Terra's. That one is followed by a couple more. I turn, preparing myself to lay into them, too, but they're not laughing at me. They're focused on Rayann.

Rayann opens and closes her mouth a few times in shock. It's an excellent impersonation of Mr. Whiskers. "Pirate ship? What are you… Ugh. Whatever! If you want to commit social suicide, be my guest." She throws her arms in the air and stomps off.

Dan stops her before she gets too far and tries to sell her a T-shirt. "Come on, Capri. It's for a good cause."

She just slaps the shirt out of his hand and keeps walking.

He turns to me and grins. "What did I say?"

• • •

The festival is a success. In fact, it exceeds my expectations. Next year, we're definitely going to need more room.

Unfortunately, the squad couldn't do a pyramid for Vera during our last performance because Rayann decided to leave. I'd like to think this whole thing might've taught her a lesson, or at least, given her something to think about, but I'm not holding my breath.

Dan and Jonah did a great job of selling the T-shirts and fan spritzers. They set up in the library parking lot so they were the first booth people came across. Surprisingly, Dan went above and beyond when it came to hocking his merchandise.

"Stay cool and help the school, get your water gun fans here!"

"All T-shirt proceeds go to charity. Show your friends how philanthropic you are! And maybe even get a tax break!"

Mom and Dad showed up later. Dad got some back issues of comics he used to read, and Mom bought a new rocking chair from the carpenter's booth.

Even Tommy, a.k.a. Sorenson, showed up in costume to sell college students on the greatness of LARP of Ages. Martha made a ton of money off the theater crowd, especially the improv troop.

All day the college station's broadcast has been piped out over our little shindig. So, when Logan pulls his mom over for a live interview toward the end of the festival, my ears perk up to listen.

"So, Martha, this festival has been awesome. What do you think?"

"I agree. We've worked really hard to make it great so this is just wonderful, Awesome Logan," Martha says.

"What gave you the idea to put this together?" His tone

sounds like he already knows the answer.

"As much as I'd like to take the credit, this wasn't my idea."

"Wait," he says, all hint of knowing the answer gone. "You told me this was your doing."

"I'm sorry. I lied." From where I'm standing on the practice mats the coach set up for the cheerleaders, I can see the trademark Scott smile spread across her face. "The truth is this was all thought up by a certain nice, young girl." She looks in my direction and Logan's gaze follows.

I pretend to be completely enraptured by the nearby bakery booth that's selling cake-pops. After a few seconds of silence, I glance back. Martha and Logan have their hands over their mics and are leaning close to each other, having what looks like a very fast-paced conversation. Martha says something that makes Logan's mouth drop open and his eyes sort of glaze over, and then she flicks him on the forehead. He sits up straight and adjusts his mic.

The sound of him clearing his throat crackles through the speakers. "Well, let's get the real mastermind mind over here. I hope all of my regular listeners remember Wonderful Wendy." He waves a hand for me to come over.

I shake my head vigorously, but Terra laughs and shoves me toward his booth. Reluctantly, I take Martha's seat. She pats my head, then leaves to help a customer.

Logan stares at me, his shock still obvious, then seems to realize we're on the air. He clears his throat again. "So, this is quite an amazing undertaking, especially for a seventeen-year-old. What made you do it?"

"I...I know this guy whose family owns a small business here in town. They were having troubles like a lot of locally owned stores, and I couldn't understand why they weren't getting the customers they deserved. I know prices are lower at the bigger, chain stores, but I think the benefits to the community are worth the extra dollar or two. Then I thought maybe people just didn't know about all the amazing stores around town. So, why not give them the opportunity to explore them in one place and make a little money for charities and the college at the same time?"

I can't believe I got all that out without stumbling over every other word, especially with how intently Logan is watching my mouth.

He shakes his head slightly and looks me in the eye. "That's very noble of you. So, what's been your favorite booth today?"

"They're all great. Did you know Cajun Confections has an orange spice cupcake with hot sauce in it? So yummy. But I'd have to say my favorite has been The Phoenix. I spent most of my money there. I picked up the first five issues of the new Green Lantern."

"I'm glad to hear it. Well, thanks for talking with me today, Wonderful Wendy, and to all the listeners—"

"Actually, my name isn't Wendy," I blurt out. "It's Maddie. Madelyne Jean Summers. I'm a cheerleader at Natchitoches Central. And I love comics."

Logan raises an eyebrow. "Good for—"

"Oh, and role-playing games. And video games." Now that I'm confessing, I can't seem to stop.

"Okay, well—"

"And reading regular books, all kinds, and science fiction stuff. I've also been thinking of making a costume for next year's

NerdCon. Maybe Princess Leia when she was captured by Jabba the—"

Logan flips the switch on the microphone. "That's great, but we need to get back to some music now." He looks like he's trying very hard not to smile.

"What? You don't like that part? I thought all guys had a thing for Leia in that metal bikini thing."

"Of course, I like Leia in the…bikini thing. But don't announce to the city you're going to be wearing that. I can hear Dan from here making a note on his phone to get passes to S.N.C. next year. And look at Tommy and his friends. They haven't stopped staring. Tommy's grooming his fake beard, for God's sake, probably getting ready to hit on you." Logan glares at Tommy, who straightens and tucks his beard comb back into his robes.

"So, you don't want me to dress up for the con next year?"

His gaze drops to my lips again. "I didn't say that."

I can't help myself. I lean closer and whisper, "How about Power Girl? I could probably work that costume up before next year."

The rest of the festival fades away when he smiles. He opens his mouth to answer me, but I don't let him speak. Instead, I press my lips to his. He goes tense, and for a second I think he's going to pull away, but then he falls into the kiss with me. He runs his palms over my bare shoulders as I wrap my arm around his neck, and I could seriously just melt away.

When I pull back, his content sigh echoes over the speakers. Ben must have turned the mic on from the control board when the song ended, which, by the look on some of the faces around us, was a long time ago.

#31

Most of the stores have packed up their booths and gone home by the time the crickets start chirping. I hang around to help put away all The Phoenix's merchandise. At some point before the job is finished, poor little Moira zonks out in the office, so Martha, Mr. Scott, and the rest of the clan go home, leaving Logan and me to lock up the shop.

We pass each other five or six times as we lug the long, white comic boxes back to the storeroom. It feels like we're two magnets being held just close enough to almost connect, but then we're pulled apart.

"There's one more left," Logan says as we pass each other again. "Could you lock the door behind you when you come back in?"

The last box isn't that heavy. It was the super cheap box so it's only half-full of one-dollar comics. I lock the front door behind me and make my way to the back room again. The sun is setting. Its pinkish-purplish rays stream in through the display windows, but the light doesn't reach the back.

I turn the corner to the back room and try to find the light switch with my elbow. I can't find it, but suddenly, the light pops on. Logan's right next to me, which scares the bejesus out of me. I squeal and drop the box. The books scatter across the floor.

"Sorry," he says. "I was trying to be smooth and help. But once again, I screw it up."

We both kneel down to gather up the comics. "What do you mean 'once again'?"

"I screwed up that day with Eric."

"That was my fault. You didn't screw anything up." My hands shake as I stack the books. "I'm sorry, Logan." I let out a long sigh. It feels like I've been waiting to say that for years.

He doesn't belittle my apology by brushing it off, by saying anything like, "It's okay, it's no biggie." He lets it hang in the air for a long minute, then nods, accepting it.

"I did mess up last night, though," he says. "Where did you go?"

I give up on trying to concentrate on the comics. "I went home. Where did you go?"

"I knew I should have told you before I left, but everything was so crazy. I went to my house to get something for you, but you were gone by the time I got back to Tommy's." He reaches over to get my notebook that was lying on one of the boxes. I didn't even notice it was there.

He holds it out to me. "Thanks," I say as I thumb through the pages. There's now green writing along with my purple throughout it.

I stop on one page: *The Super Ones* #328. Underneath where I wrote, *Marcus is such a jerk! Can't he tell Wendy loves him?* Logan wrote, in his neat, precise scrawl, *How is Marcus supposed to know if she doesn't tell him? He has plasma powers, not telepathy.*

"I hope you don't mind that I put a few things in there." He scoots closer so he can read over my shoulder.

I shake my head, too busy reading all the green ink I can find and trying to focus past my sheer delight at him being so close to me. I flip to the #400 entry.

Purple: *"Be true to yourself and others will be true to you, too." Yeah right, what a crock.*

Green: *I'd be true to you no matter what.*

I look at him over my shoulder. He's smiling that honest smile.

"Are you sure about that?" I ask. "I'm not exactly the most stable person. I'm still getting used to this whole being myself thing and—"

"I know what type of person you are. You're the girl who picked the longest book Mrs. Mackley listed in ninth grade Honors English to do a report on because it mentioned a love story on the back. You're the girl who, in tenth grade, told Elinor Pensky that if it were up to you she would have gotten the last spot on the squad. I know because she told me."

"She knew every one of our cheers. She studied them like they were her Advanced Chemistry notes."

"But everyone knew there was no way she was going to make it, seeing as her and her group of friends are known as the Nerd Herd. I mean, who does stuff like that?"

He brushes a piece of my hair that's fallen from my ponytail over my ear, his fingers lingering on the sensitive spot behind my earlobe. Despite the heat, a shiver runs across my neck. I turn and lean into him. He plants his lips firmly against mine and wraps his arms around me, pulling me to him. We stay like that for a very long time. I run my hands through his already messy hair. His hands drift up my back, and I don't care that the itchy fabric of my cheerleader top is scratching my skin even more, because he's the reason. He's the reason for a lot of things these days.

Eventually, it gets to the point where I have to come up for air. I clutch his Power Girl T-shirt and grin. "Do you need telepathy to understand that?"

"I think I get the message, but I can't be sure, really. Maybe you should tell me again."

And that's how I ended up making out with the love of my life in the storeroom of a comic shop where, it turns out, heaven really can be found.

Oh crap, did I just say "love"?

Yes, yes, I did.

acknowledgments

Thank you to the entire Entangled team for being amazing. Special thanks to my editor, Heather Howland, for taking a chance on my little story and for being brilliant. Without you, this wouldn't be happening. And thanks to Sue Winegardner, assistant editor, for being there every time I popped up on Gchat. And for being British, because that made me feel fancy. Thanks to Heather Riccio for being a ninja.

Thanks to the entire online book community. The support from bloggers, critique partners, and Twitter friends was invaluable. Thanks to the readers because without you this whole thing would have been kind of pointless, right? Thanks to the WrAHM ladies who were always there to offer opinions, friendly commiseration, and the occasional half-naked man. To my friends, Kallie Cooper and Mary Lou Solomon, for reading and telling me that it didn't suck. Thank you to Melissa Dezendorf for the encouragement and the wine. To my friends, Joey Dezendorf and Andrew Chandler, for being the perfect inspirations for a certain foul-mouthed geek. To Rodney and Sharon Miller for never, ever complaining about taking the kids for a weekend.

Thank you to Stefanie Gaither, the best JHFP critique partner/writing buddy I could ever ask for. I feel extremely lucky to have you around, gurly worm. My writing would not be what it is without you. For Bradbury, my friend.

Thank you to Patrick McPhearson for being the voice of reason a lot of times and for the encouragement. To Robin McPhearson for telling me it reminded you of a John Hughes film without me even having to prod you. Clair Bear, thanks for reading and being your loving self. Brian McPhearson, thank you for my lifetime love of comics, for always listening to my rants, and for never letting me feel too sorry for myself. Thanks to my amazing, there-are-no-words-for-how-awesome-you-are boys. I love you. Also, I promise to make a decent dinner tonight and not resort to frozen pizza.

To my husband, Shane Miller. Thank you for believing in me. There's no way I can ever express my gratitude for your support, love, and patience in words, so I'll just try to *show* every day for the rest of my life. I love you.

To my mom, Nancy McPhearson. You're the strongest person I've ever known. Thank you for supporting me, for keeping me grounded, and for making me reach for the stars. There's not much I can say that you don't already know. I love you. Also, answer your phone.

To my dad, Clyde McPhearson. You might not have been here for this crazy ride, but you were, in a sense. You told me once that I could do anything I wanted to. I never forgot that, not for a second. To know your courage, humor, and intelligence is a gift that I cherish. But mostly, thank you for you. I miss you and love you.